THE SPECTATOR

Also by Timothy Balding

The Man Who Couldn't Stop Thinking: A Novel
The Impostors: A Novel
The Zucchini Conspiracy: A Novel of Alternative Facts

THE SPECTATOR

A NOVEL

TIMOTHY
BALDING

UPPER WEST SIDE PHILOSOPHERS, INC.

NEW YORK

Upper West Side Philosophers, Inc. provides a publication venue for original philosophical thinking steeped in lived life, in line with our motto: philosophical living & lived philosophy.

Published by Upper West Side Philosophers, Inc.
New York, NY 10025, USA
www.westside-philosophers.com / www.yogaforthemind.us

The Spectator is published simultaneously in the UK and the USA.

Yoga for the Mind®

Library of Congress Cataloging-in-Publication Data

Names: Balding, Timothy, 1954- author.
Title: The spectator : a novel / Timothy Balding.
Description: New York : Upper West Side Philosophers, Inc., 2023.
Identifiers: LCCN 2023037244 (print) | LCCN 2023037245 (ebook) | ISBN 9781935830764 (paperback) | ISBN 9781935830771 (e-book)
Subjects: LCGFT: Detective and mystery fiction. | Psychological fiction. | Novels.
Classification: LCC PR9105.9.B35 S64 2023 (print) | LCC PR9105.9.B35 (ebook) | DDC 823/.92--dc23/eng/20231205
LC record available at https://lccn.loc.gov/2023037244
LC ebook record available at https://lccn.loc.gov/2023037245

Design: UWSP, Inc.
Cover Art & Design: Rui Ricardo / Folio Art

A UWSP Original Softcover

"To become the spectator of one's own life ...
is to escape the suffering of life ..."

—Oscar Wilde, *The Picture of Dorian Gray*

"You have heard me speak at sundry times of an oracle or sign which comes to me ... This sign, which is a kind of voice, first began to come to me when I was a child. It always forbids, but never commands me to do anything which I am going to do."

—Socrates, on trial, in the *Apology* of Plato

THE SPECTATOR

Foreword from the Publishers

It recently came to light that Roger P., the convicted double killer who escaped from BM prison six months ago and remains at large, left a thick volume of notes in his cell that detectives have painstakingly examined in the hope of finding clues to the fugitive's current intentions and whereabouts. Among the frivolous and absurd claims, demands, insults and declarations made by P. in these papers is a 'solemn promise' that he will surrender to the police if our company (as the biggest press in the country) publishes this manuscript—without a single change of any kind and specifically leaving untouched any 'semicolons or adverbs their editors foolishly deem superfluous.' It goes without saying that we would never normally contemplate ceding to blackmail to publish a book, let alone abandon our editorial responsibilities in such a way, if the police, advised by psychologists, did not insist that Roger P. remains a grave danger to the public and must be returned to their custody. We bring out this edition uniquely as a contribution to the common good, all the while disclaiming any approval or support for its contents—notably its slanderous judgements on our nation and its citizens—and even less evaluating any literary merit it might or might not possess.

For reasons best known to himself, P. has obviously tried to craft this tale of his as one might write a serious work of fiction, though you may be troubled by the absence of chapters, the arbitrarily interspersed and facetious subheadings, and, above all, the manner in which the author alternately refers to himself in the first and third person, while constantly shifting his tenses around, writing the past in the present and even giving the impression that some of the events in his narrative are actually taking place at a time when we know he was under lock and key. We leave it up to readers to determine for themselves whether this unreliable narrator can be believed, or even understood, and whether this is indeed fiction or contains any reality at all.

There appear to be two voices in Roger P.'s disturbed mind (at different points the writer talks about himself as 'The Spectator' — and has insisted that we give this title to the book). When all is said and done, we shall most probably have to leave it to the psychiatric community in the weeks and months to come to make head or tail of this dubious individual's story. In the meantime, we can only hope that he keeps his word and gives himself up or, failing that, that he is quickly apprehended and incarcerated so that he can do no more harm.

Readers should be aware that a substantial part of our sales revenues from this edition will be given to the families of the killer's victims.

{Unedited Manuscript Found in Roger P.'s Prison Cell}

The Spectator

Two men in my mind do dwell,
one bound for heaven, the other for hell

He's angry again. Working himself into a right old state. It was predictable, and tiresome for everyone, especially for him. In my case, these eruptions fuel only a certain resignation and the usual questions. Why did he once more fly off the handle? What more could I have done to prevent it? Have I not lectured him enough? And, of course, the real heart of the matter: Will persuasion never change him? Do I actually have to break the man?

"You promised me you wouldn't climb on the roof!" he yelled at Sandra. "What if you'd slipped and broken your neck?"

He was not exaggerating about that, it must be said; it had been a real possibility. A loose tile and she would have plunged over the gutter, smack onto the concrete two floors below.

I had helped him win the promise, offered him some of the rational arguments to use, after the parasol had been swept away by the wind and he failed to see how he could retrieve it. At the same time, I knew his wife did not take her word seriously in such matters and would clamber over the hot roof as soon as he turned his back.

The story should have ended there, with the successful rescue of the stranded parasol, a wife in one piece, laughs and congratulations all round. But he had other things in mind. Principles, morals, promises, truth, loyalty, all that dodgy piety injected into his brain lobes as a child. He had to make a point. A man had to take a stand. Clint Eastwood had taught him that at the Saturday matinées.

Perhaps only I take his real measure? Only I see how absurd he is? Others, including his wife, I suppose, most certainly find him irritating when he behaves in this way. But more than that? After all, it's typical of people who have a little temperament and character to let off steam. And who wants to be with a silent and well-behaved dullard anyhow?

I know the little fellow inside out, of course; I'm thoroughly used to him, as I should be after all these years. If truth be told, as it should be, it should probably be said that he preceded me. Though that is an unresolved chicken and egg riddle and one we shall doubtless have to return to.

In any case, here he is. A right song and dance. Raising his voice to block Sandra's attempts to speak over his din (as he often does with me), ready to increase the volume to crush any words she might *get in edgeways*, as they say. You put both of us at risk, he begins. Where could I find an ambulance at this hour, supposing that you had survived the fall? Do you realize it was I who would have had to scrape your body off the driveway? Why did you betray me? And saving the most dramatic for the end: *I shall never trust you again!*

She was patient with him, though not visibly contrite. Indeed, I'm not sure how seriously she takes all this, having been on the end of his trivial wrath quite often now. Perhaps it's merely a little entertainment for her? Her stubborn refusal to explain anything makes it difficult to say. But either way, we'll have a little chat in a quiet moment later, he and I, and examine these threats about trust to see if they have any meaning whatsoever or if they are merely rhetorical sabre-rattling, as I suspect. After all, you don't lose trust in someone over a stupid story of a parasol on a roof. At least, I don't think so.

I have to confess one thing right away, though, as we embark on our story. It's he not I who gets to decide these matters *in fine*, at the end of the day, however much I may occasionally give the impression that I am in control, that I have power over *him*. After all, I am writing this story, and not him, so a little self-aggrandisement may be expected. In any case, to a certain extent these impressions are not without some truth. More and more each day, in fact. At least I like to believe it, despite regular lapses on his part like the parasol hysteria.

But (and I would ask you, dear reader, to pay particular attention here): When all is said and done, a man feels what he feels. Even if he's lying, to himself and anybody else within earshot; even if the grounds for his outbursts are spurious, figments of his imagination; even if he is merely striking out, for complex reasons which could be examined if one had the appetite for it, in order to wound the other; even if he does not in truth *really* feel what he actually claims to feel—injured, betrayed, cheated, taken for a fool, morally outraged, persecuted, whatever—his sentiments, in the instant, of anger, of rage, are as genuine and true as the nose on his face. Surely not? Surely his absurd emotional contortions and chest beating are mere theatrics? Not at all. Imposture takes on the reality of its own lies to the point where it is indistinguishable from the *real thing*, not only in its outward appearance, for the others, but in its actual existence for the impostor.

This needs more explanation? I'll do that as our story moves along, I promise you. But for the moment, let me just insist again: A man feels what he feels and there's nothing that you or I or anyone else can do about it. This is a very important matter, on whose understanding the future of humanity may depend. Haha! The grandeur of that claim makes you laugh? All the better. We are here on this blessèd earth also to laugh, that's for sure. It's perhaps even the most important thing that we can do. It is practically my raison d'être. Not to mention that it's also my only real defence against him.

The 'People's Voice'. Tra-la-la!

He's a journalist. On one of those huge-circulation tabloids that daily soil the souls of their readers and the image of the nation. 'Hack' would be a more accurate description of his particular branch of this noble profession; but if you don't *pretend* to take your work seriously, in name at least, how can you expect to gain a minimum of respect from the world? Would 'The Daily Hack', if it were so called, still be bought by more than a million punters, not even to mention the countless masses who float in and out of the newspaper's online site on a tide of *clickbait*, a rather unpleasant term, I agree, but no less appropriate and true for that? Who knows, really? It would be good to put my hunch about the name to the test, but that's unlikely to happen, since great sums of money are involved. The owners of his and other tabloids are not in the game for laughs, let alone to convey honest information and analysis, God forbid.

I have an idea: let's call his paper 'The Daily Hack' anyhow, for the purposes of this tale. In that way, I won't be unfairly stigmatizing just one set of the moral dregs who work for these rags but can encompass them all in my odium.

Roger—yes, let's give him his name, since we can't just go on calling him 'he', can we?—joined the 'Hack' practically from school. He had no knowledge that might predispose him to gain his living in the journalistic calling, in the business of enlightening the nation and its citizens about the affairs of the world, but he had a way with words, with the pen. His language was stylistically beautiful, everyone remarked it, even when he was writing rubbish, which was more often than not the case. I wonder where on earth this unmerited skill came from and can only conclude that it was in his genes, because he had made no effort at all to study or cultivate it, didn't read much, and didn't pay much if any attention to how other people expressed themselves, either. It's like having a musical ear; you just have it or you don't. In the newsroom, he found himself in the company of a lot of old men and women who had been juggling with words all their lives. They all wrote like pigs still; hadn't improved a jot from practice. They couldn't 'hear' a good phrase if it was blasted into their ears with a megaphone.

Young and willing (and having no choice about the matter anyhow), he was at first given the dirty jobs that lay behind the acquisition of most stories in the tabloids and particularly in 'The Daily Hack'. Invading the privacy and misery of unfortunate citizens who had become the victims of crime or tragedy was high on his daily diary duties. He did not, of course, see his activities in this light. He had with ease embraced the cant that had forged and kept alive the bogus moral code of his brethren. 'The public's right to know'; 'the interests of society'; the opportunity for the abused and injured 'to tell their side of the story'; 'the demand for justice'; the 'debt' these poor bastards 'owed to the memory of their loved ones'; and other vacuous tra-la-la.

In his early tasks as a reporter, he had often barged his way into the homes of parents whose children had—in the best of cases, from the paper's point of view—been stabbed, tortured or shot to death, to obtain a photograph of the victim or, faced with the reluctance of the grieved to part with such a precious personal object and his failure to overcome their resistance with his fancy moral rhetoric, to filch one off the sitting room mantelpiece.

You ask, with good reason: Is he (or rather was he at the time, since he soon went on to more advanced kleptocracy and sin) a 'monster', to use one of 'The Daily Hack's' own favourite epithets for any wretched deviant in society who has given in to some disgusting, fatal impulse and been apprehended? Well, everything in the affairs of man is relative as far our disapprobation and condemnation is concerned, isn't it? A Middle East potentate can make *charcuterie* out of an opponent and feed him to the palace dogs and, on the condition he owns vast quantities of oil or gas and, into the bargain, will buy scores of our latest missiles, blind eyes are right now readying themselves to be turned, not least by 'The Daily Hack'. After a decent pause for appearances, or a token nod to morality, of course. So, our reporter can be considered to be in a really very minor league of indecent behaviour and rather rare it is that anyone ever has the mind to turn against him personally. Yes, yes, you say—but how about *your* judgement in the matter, and not that of the eternally tolerant and docile public, from whom we can expect little durable outrage and shock about these or any other matters in our times?

An excellent question!

I would say that he clearly has *no* excuse, none at all, but that if pressed I could come up with some mitigating circumstances. You press me? The pleasure is mine. Where do we start? I know: Man has free will. (No dialectician will ever talk me out of *that*!). At the same time, the range within which he can exercise this will is most definitely circumscribed by a number of factors. Most essentially, his birth-given personality characteristics, among them his *faculty for passion,* about which far, far too little is ever spoken (practically nothing, in fact) when you consider its impact on our lives and those of the others. Yes, a man is born with a certain level of passion. In some people, it is barely discernible at all, of course. Take the average Englishman. No, no, I'm joking, we must not go in that direction, however tempting it might be. Anyhow, this powerful instinct of passion, when it exists, can drive a man in many directions, the majority of which we might consider as good, a few others distinctly less so. Most passionate people, even though otherwise well disposed for it, could not become serial killers, for instance, not least from a lack of time between the family and the office. This is why they are so rare, happily. A great deal of passion and, of course, single-mindedness and ambition, not to mention countless spare hours, are needed to become such a 'beast', to pluck another word from the tabloid hack's lexicon.

So, along what other, more wholesome, paths might passionate natures charge? They could be of a creative nature, for example, splashing themselves across canvasses, filling the pages of a dozen novels, flooding the air with delightful music, making great scientific discoveries about the universe, becoming skilful lovers, or designing the flying automobiles of the future. It is not for us, not right now at least, and perhaps not at all, to judge the usefulness to humanity of such of passion's objectives.

But let us not forget what one could well argue is the most important of such endeavours. Passion harnessed to great ideas! Passion in the quest for understanding, for insight, for knowledge, for truth. Passion to see reason and justice triumph in the world, perhaps? Passion to improve humanity! For without these passions, it's clear man will forever remain in his cave, however prettily he has otherwise decorated it and with whatever gadgets and entertainment he may occupy his time, or, failing to be absorbed by such diversions, be tempted to go and torture, rape and kill those in the next cave in an effort to overcome his boredom. It happens somewhere every day; look around you, my friends.

This yearning for truth, reason and justice, rather unequally shared between men, like all passions, comes from where, you ask? Does it just fall from the heavens into some men's laps and not others? Well, I can tell you its origin in Roger's case, if you like, but only if you will be patient and listen still (I know I promised you a *story*; it's coming, don't fret). And perhaps you might just be persuaded to caress the idea that it may also be how all of us who long for reason's victory upon our sacred earth became similarly endowed. In the absence of credible alternatives to explain its existence, of course ...

The source of the desire for reason and justice *lies in the understanding that 2+2 equals 4. And, no less so, in your accept-*

ance for once and always that it is thus and nothing else, and your absolute determination to defend this truth to the death. No! Surely you jest, Sir? Not at all. Despite Dostoevsky's excellent quip that it would be most charming to conclude that 2+2 equals 5, it does not. I would even contend that if you think *that,* you have embarked on a sinister adventure where everything is possible, perhaps even the very worst.

Roger's fate was to fall deeply in love with this equation the very first time he grasped it. Up until that moment, he believed nothing and no one, to the point where his parents, faced with his stubborn refusal to accept without question anything at all they ever said or did (he refused even to eat his food before one of his parents first tasted it, like a king of old—or a modern dictator—afraid to be poisoned), began to think that they had given birth to a sceptic.

Then 2+2 came into this obtuse boy's life; at nursery school, it was. A teacher had distributed two chocolate biscuits to all of the class and said, "Daddy has given you two biscuits" (though he thought this rather stupid, since Daddy was off working in an office somewhere, as far as he knew). She had hastily continued: "Do not eat them yet, children! Because Mummy is also going to give you two chocolate biscuits!" He had looked round the class for his mother, but she wasn't there either. (Later in life, it would dawn on him that he took things too literally, a handicap that, with my help, he was eventually able to remedy). They all sat there silently on the floor, Roger and his classmates, with their sweaty hands outstretched, each hand gripping two chocolate biscuits, which instantly began to melt and make a fine mess. But the teacher wasn't finished. "So, children, you have two biscuits from your father, and two biscuits from your mother. Remember our adding lesson. How many biscuits do you have?"

"Four!" screamed Roger, startling the other boys and girls before they had even had time to think about the question.

"Yes!" exclaimed the teacher. "Roger is right! Well done,

Roger! Because two plus two equals four!" And then, solemnly, she added: "You must never forget this, children, for it will serve you well in life, indeed will perhaps be the most important thing you ever learn," catching her breath in the emotion of the moment or because she suspected that she had perhaps gone too far with this advanced pedagogical notion.

Roger was very pleased indeed, almost ecstatic. Not because he had been the first to come up with the answer (he was not unduly competitive), nor that it allowed his grateful mates to finally cram the biscuits into their mouths without further ado. Unlike them, he did not move a muscle. His fingers dripping with chocolate, his arms still in the air, he looked stunned. He vaguely heard the mistress enquire, "Roger?," but he was elsewhere. He did not know it then, of course, but he was having a mathematical epiphany of great beauty and consequence. His little brain could not articulate what he felt, but he sensed it anyhow: Finally, something in his existence was sure and certain and he somehow knew that it would remain so forever. It was unquestionable, incontrovertible; all doubt in his life vanished in its blinding light; for better or worse, he would forever be enchained to its inevitability. And despite the countless wild-goose chases on which he would later embark in search of some meaning to his existence, it would eventually put him on the right road, this 2+2 equals 4, this founding stone of man's reason and justice, his two greatest contributions to life in all of its manifestations on earth and presumably also in heaven. Amen.

In recounting this little anecdote from Roger's early years, I have actually neglected what I believe might be its most important dimension: That it was doubtless in that classroom among the sweaty children and the chocolate biscuits that I myself was born or, at least, made my very first appearance.

And as you digest the magnitude of our hero's epiphany, perhaps you will begin to see, as I did—still do?—that there may be some salvation for him therein, if not redemption. Or at least a new trial ...? In any case, after a suitable pause for thought about that, let us continue briefly with our narrative of the man's childhood.

Hail the great unbeliever!

Roger was bursting from infancy with passion, but no one, alas, ever suggested in which direction he might aim it, for they did not recognize it for what it was—people rarely do—and, to be honest, cared even less. Teachers had a job to do, after all, and could not dwell on the personalities and temperaments of every child! Perhaps herein lies the tragedy of education, when all is said and done? So much promise left by the wayside because of the lack of attention and of individual psychological diagnosis (and thus perhaps remedy?), even of the most elementary kind? As for parents, for the *home environment,* as they call it, let's face the facts: while society endlessly examines and laments—and rightly so—the nefarious effects of broken and abusive childhoods on those who grow up with criminal or otherwise anti-social tendencies (not to mention those, absolutely innocent, whose behaviour is beyond reproach but who sink into mental misery and despair), it keeps very quiet about the genesis of the complete scoundrels, our bent politicians, for example, or the slave masters exploiting the workers in our factories, or the designers of lethal weapons, whose infancies played themselves out on sweet-smelling beds of roses.

I digress again. It will not be the last time, I forewarn you. But I have, my friends, the blessings of Laurence Sterne, who wrote in *Tristram Shandy*: "Digressions, incontestably, are the sunshine; they are the life, the soul of reading." You see, Roger and I have been doing our homework, working our way around the literary giants. It's most rewarding, I must say. We are definitely the richer for it. Anyhow, the temptation of digression is compelling when we look at what's happening around us and have an ardent desire to right the wrongs in the world on the basis of reason and justice, a much better bet than the foolish belief of pop singers and priests that preaching 'love' is the road to anywhere at all and will prevent or even delay our eventual perdition. No, ladies and gentlemen! Neither hope of love nor kindness, nor a world without possessions, nor the abolition of countries, nor some imaginary brotherhood of man (as one of our late *chanteurs*, a self-confessed wifebeater living in a Manhattan penthouse, once gibberized), none of this prattle, though the whole world sing along with it, will ever change a single thing about our future. But reason and justice, on the other hand, 2+2 equals 4, they may just give us a slim chance of getting out of the mess we have created for ourselves …

In Roger's case, struggling to find something particular to say about him, as they were obliged to do with every child, some of whom in truth they barely noticed, the teachers wrote in their reports that he was 'vociferous'. They did not mean this unkindly, though a few were sometimes led in exasperation to bluntly order him to "shut up" as he tried once more to explore his own thoughts out loud in front of the whole class. In the end, of course, finding no interest or echo for his struggle to make sense of the world through the prism of his new mathematical dogma, he did precisely that. He fell silent and for years afterwards plotted his way out of this childhood prison into a world where people would surely be more interested in having an argument with him.

Thus Roger's passion just existed, in a vacuum, if you like, unattached to anything. And, like other powerful and doubtless antediluvian instincts in a man's breast—love, hate, envy, jealousy, fear, lust—eventually turned upon itself in the absence of a worthwhile object and became a source first of frustration and later of self-loathing. But more of that anon …

Society still insists, as it has been doing for over a century now and will not give up doing except at gunpoint, that we are all the products of our schools and of our families and, if we manage at certain moments to escape their grip, we are at the very least shaped, nay, *created,* by the culture in which we grow up. Try and argue with someone who has swallowed this canon hook, line and sinker. You are wasting your breath, Sir! Listen to the *self-development* gurus and the *life coaches* who currently hold centre stage in our desperate societies. This motley crew of thieves, who in the absence of any thoughts of their own have ransacked every last scrap of paper in Buddha's bottom sock drawer (they generally avoid the less sentimental Greeks) and endlessly quote ancient Persian poetry, will invariably tell you that *nothing is impossible,* that we can all become rocket scientists or trapeze artists if only *we set our minds to it*. Though they rarely highlight the contradiction, they are at the same time the first to point accusing fingers at our parents, our educators, our friends, our enemies, for having emasculated our will and our superpowers in the first place!

No, in its articles of faith, society and the people who set the tone of its incessant gabble would have it that we cannot possibly escape our pasts. This is perhaps the case for some; we are forced to admit it. One could otherwise hardly explain all our prejudices, our religious convictions or lack of them, or our political biases, for that matter, if it were not so, could we? No one is born blabbering on about God or the Conservative Party, after all. I'd like to bet, though, that if anyone were ever able to sufficiently study the question, they would find that the men and women who do indeed unquestioningly inherit their views along with their physique or the wretched family porcelain would for the most part be people without passion. At least the rare passion for asking oneself honest questions, the passion for placing oneself in front of the judge who will ask them to justify themselves on the actual grounds of reason. Anyhow, we can hope; we must always hope. We can take a bet right here and now, if you like? That both God and the Conservative Party too will disappear into the history books, rather sooner than later as things are going. Any takers?

But where were we? Yes, I was going to come on to the men—who even many among those of us given to serious thought claim do not exist, claim are impossible—who pass through childhood without a single important idea, ambient prejudice, value, belief or conviction sticking to them. Roger was such a man. And it was he who stumbled across a clue to this enigma while distractedly surfing through one of those Top Ten (films, books, sexual positions, salads, footballers, poisonous snakes, fashion models, or whatever) lists on a national broadcaster's website that had unaccountably decided, perhaps in a moment of inattention, to raise the intellectual level of its content with a gap-filler on 'The Top Ten Quotes About Belief', an interesting subject indeed! Among those who had emitted them was Nietzsche, who I'm sure would have been greatly tickled to be listed, being not the austere thinker so many imagine, and having an enormous sense of fun and humour to boot. I savour it to this day, in any case: "Unbelief as an instinct is a precondition of greatness." So, perhaps our Roger, our own devout unbeliever, is destined for great things too? Haha! That would be a fine thing!

Timothy Balding

Life is not about stories, my friends

A story, a story, my kingdom for a story! For pity's sake, man! Let us have it! And *show don't tell*! How else can you hold a reader's attention against the distractions of the age? You've probably lost half of them already with your moralistic meanderings about the state of society and the nation. Still it is, my friends: The affairs of an age are woven into the fabric of a man's life even if they do not change or shape him or, even less, influence his nature in any meaningful manner. They do little more—though it is already too much—than occupy the space between his ears; clothe his mind, if you like, whether in finery or in rags is up to him, depending upon the direction in which he turns his attention and whether he embraces, tries to ignore, or indeed rejects that upon which his gaze falls and his hearing engages. But few are able to extract themselves completely from what is going on around them in our societies, few can avoid being sucked down into the great black hole of the piddling and the piffling. One might suspect, in fact, that this escape is really given only to idiots and hermits. And take my word for it, if you will, Roger is neither.

So, the story. If this manuscript is to see the light of day, which is my ambition, it would normally have to heed the edicts of our time and conform to what the experts think it is that people want to read (even though, as a rule of thumb in the sales profession, and a sure way of saving time and money, we are better inspired to *tell* them what they want than to try and understand any natural predispositions they might have identified for themselves). And in this respect, the gatekeepers of the land of literature, the dreaded *agents*, that powerful, impudent caste forever fighting losing battles against the unstoppable tide of words flooding their computer inboxes, have set the rules, the guidelines. We shall get strictly nowhere if we are not prepared to cut *their* mustard, to deliver the goods *they* have ordered, as we storm the drawbridges of their uninviting citadels where all the talk is of *target audiences, genres, sales hooks, social media platforms* and such like. And, my friends, we have at the very least to propose to them a *story*. With conflict, tension, suspense, a *plot*, a little violence perhaps? But I get enough of all that at home, you protest? Don't worry, don't suffer over this matter (as Roger once did after sending around his poor attempt at a detective novel): For you will be in good hands if you can get your feet in the door of *their* castles. Alternatively, of course, a clever man might cook up some devious scheme to get around them and into a publisher's enthusiastic, or indeed unwilling, embrace …

I do not like this word 'story', though. It most particularly makes me wince in the mouths of television news presenters: "A young man was arrested this morning after he killed five members of his family with a sword, decapitating his parents, then cutting his three young siblings into pieces. Over to our reporter J. C. *for the story*." And after a short report, distinctly lacking in any story at all, and an advertising break for the insurance you don't need: "Saudi warplanes bombed a Yemen school this morning, killing at least thirty-five children. F. P. *has the full story*."

Life is not about stories, children. As you will find out when you finally venture into the world on your own … But we must tell them anyhow, it seems, because nothing will ever hold together or make any sense on its own and we shall otherwise die in confusion and desperation listening to the *idiot* tell his tale. And if we don't have any story of our own worth telling, well, we shall just have to make one up, shan't we?

So, our *story*, Roger and me.

Timothy Balding

Foucault's bastards

By the time in Roger's short career about which I want to speak to you, he has, remarkably enough, become what on 'The Daily Hack' they call Investigations Editor. He leads a team of eight reporters who, day and night, stand at his beck and call to rummage through any garbage can or waste basket in the land or ferret around in the underpants or knickers of the 'Hack's' enemies. If you have left the slightest dubious trace of your sorry life on the internet, they will even more easily find your hidden trash there. As for the popular actress who unwisely sends her semen-stained sheets to the laundry company, which readily lends them to a 'Hack' reporter for a little DNA testing … This is sordid, Sir, you protest!? Yes, it is, and so is the tabloid press business in our little nation; I cannot help that.

You say *enemies*, though? You are surely not telling us that a newspaper devoted to the search for truth and virtue designates its own enemies? Oh but yes; don't be shocked. The unwritten list of our favourite tabloid's foes is as long as a dozen arms. Intellectuals, scientists, academics, judges, ecologists, foreigners, sociologists, civil servants, tofu-eating *lefties*. And authors? You must be joking! 'The Daily Hack' could not care a hoot about literature, so we are on safe ground here. Though they could destroy us in the blink of an eye, they really wouldn't take the trouble, wouldn't bother. In the first place—the only place, actually—their readers care even less for literature than they do.

Roger in turn is at the mercy of his Chief Editor's latest obsession or famous instinct for smelling a rat in any otherwise innocent event or life. This editor has two posters stuck on the wall behind his desk. One says, 'Nothing Is As It Seems'; the other, 'Everyone Has A Dirty Secret'. Hardly journalistic college stuff, I agree, but since no reporter on the 'Hack' has been within a hundred miles of such a school, which remain establishments of great mockery and derision at the tabloids, these are taken as wisdoms worthy of the highest regard.

Fred Bowdler is the man's name. He claims to be a descendant of the notorious physician Thomas Bowdler, who famously published an expurgated family edition of Shakespeare's plays 'made suitable for women and children'. There is no bowdlerisation of anything going on at the 'Hack', though, since women—who represent a large proportion of its readers—apparently no longer require protection of their virtue, it having presumably been lost at some point since the 19th century.

Bowdler is a villain of the highest order, a man who has missed out on any lessons anyone ever offered on honesty, ethics, morality or truth. He is alternately in a great rage or very kind and charming and it is at any moment difficult to see the signs that either state is approaching. This leads his staff to be very cautious indeed in his presence.

The man has a hobby which conveniently provides a constant stream of stories for his newspaper—conspiracy theories. It is said that as a child he was obsessed with Unidentified Flying Objects and would spend days and nights lying on his back in the garden hoping to spot one. As an adult and as a journalist, he lost interest in UFOs, stories of alien kidnappings and a huge range of paranormal phenomena that had been his youthful passion. Now, he devotes himself to theories that implicate *real people* and serve his profound thirst for destroying lives and reputations.

Bowdler called Roger into his office this morning and asked him what he knew about *vapour trails*. Not one ever to be caught ignorant of and unprepared for a subject that could even momentarily flit across his Chief Editor's vast mind, Roger responded: "Interesting stuff. We should be looking at them much more closely, shouldn't we chief?" *I* knew, of course, that he hadn't a clue what the chief was talking about, and was fishing for the reply that he indeed received.

"Damn fucking right!" says Bowdler. "Get onto it will you? Let me know what's the best story—that these people are fucking nutjobs and should be locked up for spreading senseless fear, or that they have a case and some evil force in the deep state is slowly poisoning us." And with that he hands a letter to Roger and waves him out of his office.

No one knows whether or not Fred Bowdler actually gives credence to any of the conspiracy theories upon which he fixes his curiosity. The fact, however, is that it shows a grotesque misunderstanding of tabloid journalism to even contemplate the question. For it supposes that you are sufficiently simple-minded as to believe that Bowdler is in any way, shape or form interested in the truth in these or any other matters. There was apparently once a time, though it may be mythical, when a man or woman who had any dealings with the public at all, an editor, a police officer, a teacher, a pastor, a politician, had to pay lip service to this *truth* business. Things were true, or they were not true. Then the psychoanalysts came along, with French philosophers soon in hot pursuit, and kicked the stuffing out of the whole idea of truth, which didn't after all exist, at least not in the way we all had thought, but was a matter of perspective; of your *unconscious* mind, perhaps; of your cultural prejudices, it went without saying; probably of your race, creed and sexual orientation into the bargain!

For Bowdler, *your* truth is just that, yours, and since he doesn't care in the slightest what you think or believe, it is of no interest to him whatsoever. 'The Daily Hack'—in other words Fred Bowdler—decides the truth and the facts and, it must be said, its readers are very happy with this arrangement, since it saves them the burdensome task of thinking about anything when they are not watching television. In all this, Bowdler is nothing exceptional, of course. Truth has long gone out of fashion in society; it was *so* tedious, my dear; now we can say and believe what on earth we want and woe betide the fool who dares to contradict us. Simply *everybody* is on our side today. If we get into a little rhetorical difficulty over the question, we can now just call any passing quantum physicist to the rescue! He'll tell you there's no reality (and thus no truth, because that requires reality) and, if you are kind to him, and he is feeling playful, will most likely justify also your suspicion that 2+2 does indeed equal 5. Not even to mention a certain American President who ruled the world for four years on the basis of whatever the hell happened to be passing through his head, true or false, and, to boot, convinced seventy-four million people to give him another run at it, a most impressive number, even if it was not quite enough.

Yes, dear readers, 2+2 equals 4, the great founding truth of civilisation as we know it, is fast being consigned to the trashbin of human history. Well, I shall just have to be the last man on the walls of truth's Alamo to defend it, shan't I?

There is, of course, a funny side to all this, though, if you can contemplate with a chuckle or two the pending extinction of the human race, as I enjoy doing (after all, it won't affect anyone we know personally, so why should you or I care in the slightest?). Here it is: Not the least ironical and comical aspect of the left-baiting, intellectual-hating, French-loathing mass audience tabloids is that the very flexible notions of truth that they share with their readers essentially owe their presence in the common human psyche to left-wing French philosophers. Fred Bowdler is Foucault's bastard son! And he hasn't even heard of him!

So, what is in the letter this child of Foucault gives to Roger?

This badly-printed missive is headed with the rather amateurish and clumsy logo of an airplane in flight pumping into the blue sky behind it the name, 'International Chemtrail Alert Association'. Oh, so that's it, thinks Roger, skimming through the content. Those fools who believe we are being sprayed with toxic products to reduce our intelligence (which one would hardly think necessary, when television is doing such a good job) with the aim of making us all more passive and compliant with the current political regime we are stuck with. Well, it might be one explanation why we are doing nothing to rid ourselves of them, it's true, don't you think?

What can I do with *this*, wonders Roger? Perhaps nothing, in the hope that Bowdler will forget all about it and move on to his next conspiracy before I bump into him again?

Why not get an expert's opinion first, I suggest to Roger? Don't forget you are due to have dinner soon with your neighbour Archie Samuels, the renowned biochemist.

Great idea, says Roger, thanking me, a rare enough thing at the time.

Notes from the Underground

Yes, as luck would have it, Roger and his wife Sandra (I'll introduce her to you properly in due course) were indeed invited to an evening with the Samuels just a few days later. A member of Roger's team was told to put together two short briefing notes for the occasion: one on the infamous chemtrails, the other, in strict confidence and for his eyes only, on Archie (one cannot openly investigate your dinner host, after all; it could be taken badly).

In truth, on his best days Roger P. could bluff his way through a conversation with Einstein and make the scientist believe that he had mastered with ease all his theories. Reasonably clever journalists—and let's not discount just quite yet that Roger has a certain *savoir faire*—can interview any man on earth (women, having on the whole less ego, are rather more difficult in this respect) and give him the impression he is chatting with a fellow expert. It was I, actually, who told Roger how to do it very early in his career. The trick is to ask simple, broad questions (even if they are not particularly piercing questions, the subject will construe them in his own mind as actually related to something complex he considers to be important), to listen attentively, never interrupt, and, above all, to keep your mouth shut and your own opinions to yourself. The result can be astonishing when a reporter manages to place his self-conceit under lock and key (something which, it is true, is very difficult for our journalists, particularly the big mouths in our tabloid media, who ceaselessly wish to inject their 'I's' into every third paragraph of everything they write or say). Anyhow, to get to the point: The universal human truth we are illustrating here is that a man likes nothing more in the whole world (and this is triply so if he is an *expert* in anything meaningful at all, like Archie, for example) than to talk about himself and what drives or obsesses him. Try it once, my friends, if you are not already a great listener, as so few people manage to be. Gain their confidence and then set the people off talking and sit back for the ride.

So it is that tonight Roger and Sandra P. are sitting down for a fine dinner with Archie and Sheila Samuels, with one of the men knowing a good deal more about the other than he could possibly suspect. It is only the second time that they have formally got together, these two couples, in this way. On the table is a feast of food from sea, field and farm which Sheila proudly assures us (not that we are in the slightest bit interested in the subject) is all either wild or *organic*.

"I suppose they would be, after all, in view of Archie's job," says Roger.

I tell him that this sounds rather sarcastic, so he wipes the smile off his face and tries to look studious and impressed.

"That's where it all came from, it's true," says Sheila.

"Archie could frighten the pants off you or at least turn your stomach with his tales of the pesticides, hormones, antibiotics, synthetic chemicals, genetic manipulation or radiation related to what's in our plates. Or rather other people's. We're completely biological, Archie and me, aren't we dear?"

Archie looks embarrassed at this idea, but gruntingly approves.

Not one to hang about when he sees an opening, and against my advice to approach the matter with a bit of stealth, my boy leaps into the breach and says in his best casual tone:

"Odd choice of words, though, this *biological,* isn't it, for untainted food? When we talk about biological *weapons,* they're the ones designed to poison and kill us."

"Yes, it's a clumsy expression," admits Archie. "But it's what we have. 'Organic' means something else again, though the two are often used indiscriminately."

"Let's not talk shop, though," Sandra pipes up. "Otherwise we'll be in for another tirade about government efforts to restrict the media, won't we Roger?"

Roger doesn't get the time to be irritated at his wife for trying to redirect the train of his questioning, which he has not discussed with her. Happily, Archie says: "Really, I don't mind. Go on, Roger."

It seems a little premature to me, frankly, but Roger takes the plunge.

"Actually, I'm working on a little piece right now which should be up your street—these so-called chemtrails. There's been a massive outbreak of calls to the police and the newspapers by folk who think they are being bombed by chemicals this summer. It's a meteorological phenomenon, isn't it, Archie? The current weather is apparently multiplying the sightings and the hysteria."

"Yes, that's about it," says Archie. "As we all know, airplanes leave trails of condensation which normally disappear as they cross the sky. These 'contrails', as they are known, are formed when water vapour and burning fuel particles freeze into crystals. They dissipate rapidly, except when humidity is high; then, they can stick around for hours and even form clouds. That's it, in short. Neither our governments nor aliens are spraying us with toxic substances in order to reduce population or pacify us, which seem to be the most popular yarns told by the conspiracists."

"And according to the letters which are now pouring into the papers, including several to my Chief Editor, they are also spreading Covid-19 or alternatively distributing vaccines through the atmosphere," adds Roger. "Take your pick on that one!"

They all laugh.

Roger sticks his hand into his trouser pocket and, for reassurance, I suppose, runs his hand over his briefing notes, as though he's reading braille. Is it the moment, he asks me? As good as any, I acquiesce.

"So, there's nothing to all this, then? I can do a short piece on mass hysteria and suggest expanding the capacity of our psychiatric wards, for the worst cases, and see if old Bowdler can use it as a filler?"

"Yes, that's pretty much it, I'm afraid," says Archie confidently.

"There's only one thing troubling me," Roger comes back. "I've looked into the history of all this, of course, and found something interesting. Did you know, Archie, that we have, *in this country,* sprayed the people with dangerous chemicals and micro-organisms in the past?"

Roger pauses; Archie smiles and shakes his head slowly from side to side, not in denial, apparently, but in admiration at our hack's knowledge.

"Oh yes. And it's not even a secret. Large parts of our blessèd isles were used as a giant laboratory for testing germ warfare—for almost forty years, it was. Didn't end, *or so they tell us,* until 1979."

Archie is clearly an intelligent fellow; he doesn't look rattled at all. He keeps smiling, and invites Roger to go on.

"What's a micro-organism, anyhow, Archie?"

"It could be a virus or a bacteria."

"So our Covid nutters are not so insane, then? We've sprayed disease all over the people before, why indeed not now?"

Roger advisedly falls silent. He's asked the questions, now is the time to make them speak …

"Where did you find all this?" asks Archie.

"Ve haf our vays," says Roger childishly, imitating an accent that we still play with, two lifetimes and a thousand films after the war. "Actually, it was in a newspaper clipping from twenty years ago, a competitor. I can't imagine why the story rather fell into history. A government testing biological weapons on its own people—i.e. us—and we've forgotten all about it. It was mainly from planes, too, that's the interesting part."

"I know what you're talking about, of course," says Archie. "I'm paid to, after all; it's broadly my field. It was all completely harmless, but necessary at a time we could have been attacked at any moment by the Soviets, who were totally immoral about such things and wouldn't have hesitated to kill us all with deadly germs."

"So we do it to ourselves, instead, is that it?"

Calm your indignant tone, Roger my boy, it's not the time. Roger obeys me, brings his voice down a few decibels and an octave, and adds, feeling up his braille sheet again:

"I understand that at least one of the trials wasn't harmless at all, Archie. For almost ten years, our planes flew up and down the country dropping, what was it, yes, *zinc cadmium sulphide* on millions of people. As you surely know, cadmium is recognised as a cause of lung cancer. A bit difficult to justify all that, don't you think?"

Bravo, Roger, you got that off pat, my boy. Keep going.

"And it was not only planes! Can you credit that military

ships just off the coast sprayed bacteria including e.coli and bacillus globigii—it's like anthrax, as you are aware—into the population over a five to ten-mile radius, exposing more than a million people to their effects. And it goes on and on. Perhaps the best was the release of bacteria in the Underground, on the northern line between Colliers Wood and Tooting Broadway, at *lunchtime,* to poison as many people as possible, we must suppose. Even the Americans were in on it, cooperating with our people in several of these *experiments*. It's all rather scandalous, don't you think, Archie?"

Sheila Samuels clearly feels her husband is in some roundabout way being personally implicated in this horrible story and intervenes:

"Truly *awful* things went on in the past, didn't they?! Thank goodness that's all behind us. I'm sure everybody was doing it, so you can't really say our people and government were worse than the others. Some more wine, Sandra?"

She starts fussing over the plates and glasses in front of us and clearly hopes that she's put an end to the whole business. Little does she know Roger P., Investigations Editor of 'The Daily Hack'.

"It *is* the Ministry of Defence you work for, isn't it, Archie? They were the '*people*' behind all this, they said it themselves."

"Not directly, no," says Archie, "I'm not a civil servant. I'm in private business, though it's true we have a permanent *relationship*, let's say, with the Ministry. And a lot of business with other countries, too, which brings us into regular contact with Foreign Affairs. But I can't tell you much beyond that, Roger; we have signed confidentiality agreements to prevent just that. As I'm sure you understand."

"So, your work is secret? Like those experiments spraying the population with disease?"

Now, it's Sandra who clearly senses the whole conversation is taking an unpleasant turn and jumps in.

"Come on Roger, take your reporter's hat off tonight, so

we can all relax. You're beginning to sound like an inquisition."

I tell Roger to bite his tongue and leave it there. I insist, in fact, that he shut down his interrogation this very moment. He starts to argue with me, tells me that this is his big opportunity, that it might not come around again soon, and so on. But he finally obeys me, thank goodness. It isn't always easy, dear reader, for me to control the man, once he's got the bit between his teeth and is in hot pursuit of his victim. It's his killer instinct (though perhaps it's unwise of me to use that particular expression in the current context. Haha!).

The subject of germ warfare and chemtrails is thus buried for the night. As you may well imagine, it will re-emerge, otherwise I shouldn't have bothered telling you all about it, of course.

A pandemic of stupidity

More often than not, Roger finds me a drag. An impediment to his unbridled instincts. A permanent trouble-maker. A killjoy. That's just tough, isn't it? In fact, we have developed a love-hate relationship, as the saying goes. Mainly one of hate, as far as he's concerned. It seems as though I am making the poor boy unhappy, destroying his self-confidence, undermining what he thinks he knows about life and the world, or at least what he has up until now assumed he could get by with. For my part, as the years go by, I am slowly warming to him. With however much reluctance and backsliding, he knows he has to change. He has even pretty much admitted it to me. That's what I like about him. At the back of his head, 2+2 is as active as ever; he has perhaps tried to forget it, incompatible as truth, justice and reason find themselves with the exercise of tabloid journalism, but we both know he cannot rid himself of it now, that it's too late.

At first, in his early twenties (he's just now turned thirty), when I finally found my voice after years of watching him in silent horror, Roger couldn't understand why I kept interfering in his life. Can't a man just say what he thinks and do what he wants, he'd ask me, without an observer peering over his shoulder and passing judgement on everything? It's true, in those days I rarely spoke to him in a complimentary fashion. He hadn't even *begun* to deserve it, let's be clear. In the early days, I limited myself to questions, those little devils we can place in a man's mind, on the condition it's open for business, of course, and which in time create more trouble than unpleasant truths spoken outright. During his conversations with his love interests (before he married Sandra, that is), with his colleagues, or with friends, even indeed with his informers and the victims of his 'Hack' stories, I developed the routine of butting in when he least expected it and asking disconcerting things like:

Do you have any idea what you're talking about?

Do you have any evidence for this assertion?

Why do you say something so palpably false? You know you're lying, don't you?

Have you the beginning of a clue about how extraordinarily ignorant you are?

Why do you continue to spout the latest rubbish you overheard about this subject? Won't you think for yourself—or at least look into it a little more deeply?

Occasionally, I would also meddle in the conduct of his affairs and go beyond my initially limited ambition of helping him understand himself (as far as that is possible for any man, of course, and the jury is still out on that one, though I'm not sure why) and to realize that he was essentially living on quicksand.

You have no future with this girl, it's clear, I would tell him. *Why don't you leave her alone? Find someone more suitable to you and her both? This is all going to end in a complete mess, can't you see that? Perhaps even blood on the walls. Probably yours.*

And, closer to his heart even than women: *This hack racket in which you are fast making yourself a star — is this 'true' life? Is this getting you closer to any knowledge about existence, about the human condition? Or could it just be a playground for fools and liars, hermetic, completely cut off from reality? Why do you and your mates labour under the illusion that you are the centre of the living world? After all, no other profession in which we engage, with the possible exception of politics, believes itself to be at the heart of human endeavour, does it?*

Give it some thought, Roger, won't you? I kept urging him, as he tried, and usually failed, to silence my questions, often by drowning me in whisky, and sometimes just by humming to himself, which permits no thought at all, of course. Try it if you don't believe me.

I often told Roger that he would one day have to make up his mind. That he couldn't put the decision off forever, wouldn't be able to bluff it out with himself indefinitely. That he was perfectly free to stride on through this cruel world in the brutish fellowship of the crooks and the compromised with the blind and thoughtless insouciance with which he had begun life after his liberation from childhood's chains. But I warned him too that if he did so, a moment, a day of reckoning, if you like, would surely come when his counterfeit world would collapse like a Potemkin village in a tempest. It was on this occasion that he first told me to go to hell, but I said that I had no intention at all of making that voyage with him.

Roger thought that I was being unnecessarily dramatic about it all. He was sure that his abyssal ignorance of the finest accomplishments of mankind in thought, in the arts, in science, could not possibly prove a handicap. He had never been challenged about it, for a start. The modern panoply of an average man's knowledge stretches at best from sport to cinema and it is far more useful for him to be familiar with the latest news about these matters than to be able to cite from Aristotle! Would Roger be happy if he determinedly held his course, though, and obliterated all these questions for ever from his internal dialogue, from his conscience (it's clear I would have to go down with the ship, too, but there will be other men to save, of course)? Well, we don't know, do we? Only one thing is sure—no one will notice; no one will hold him to account. Nothing at all is any longer expected of anyone in our times in terms of his awareness and knowledge. Renaissance man is today a matter for the history books and the occasional television series, as we lurch on full throttle towards a mindlessness even the educated classes have not before known.

At this time when I began to torment Roger with questions, I encouraged him to turn to reading. Just a few classics to start, and the odd philosophical work, perhaps? He couldn't see the point. It was a lot of effort, wasn't it? And the fruits, if indeed there were any, were totally useless to get about in life. No one he knew personally had the faintest knowledge of such matters. He couldn't go down to the pub after work and start talking about Joyce or Spinoza, could he? Not in this country, at any rate. A recent Prime Minister, educated at the most celebrated public school and then the top university, no less, had been humiliated on prime time American television—and *that* takes a lot of doing, believe me—when under questioning he confessed that he didn't know what *Magna Carta* meant 'in English'. One of the founding documents of our sacred nation and the bozo didn't have a clue! So much for education and culture in our fair isles. Who needs it today, my friends? Apart from everybody.

We fought about it for a long time, as Roger went about his daily business of creating phoney scandals, pillorying 'The Daily Hack's' enemies, and gratuitously promoting the proprietor's political darlings of the moment. I suggested, for example, that the prime purpose of gaining some culture might not be that of sustaining conversations with innkeepers. Perhaps Roger might do it for himself, for his own benefit? So that our own chats might become more interesting, richer, perhaps? Or even—and here I think I was rather clever—to arm him better against my relentless inquisition? He said he would take my reflections into consideration ...

One day, while reading one of the more upmarket newspapers, mainly with the objective of stealing a story idea or two, Roger wandered by accident into the book pages and fell upon a little idea from Jonathan Swift that struck him forcefully, forever an encouraging sign for a thinking man: "It is useless to attempt to reason a man out of a thing he was never reasoned into," said the Irishman.

That's true, isn't it Roger? I asked him. Good job you don't have any opinions or ideas which are actually your own—you are a free man on that score!

He didn't at all like me saying this, even in jest. No one likes to be told that he doesn't have any truly *personal* ideas, no opinions that he has actually formulated for himself through the process of thinking. No, that could really upset a man. As indeed it did Roger.

For my part, I wondered if Swift's truth, spoken almost three hundred years ago, might just explain the massive, unparalleled pandemic of stupidity that has broken out world wide now that each and every man and woman has the means to broadcast his or her thoughts to the entire planet. Although, now I think about it, it may be precisely why we no longer try and persuade anybody of anything, finding it a lot less stressful and tiring simply to insult them.

I'm sure you think that I was too hard on the man, don't you, ladies and gentlemen? In my defence, I must say that there were moments that I became a little afraid for him myself and took pity, took a little time off the job, as it were. Shattering a man's self-confidence must be approached with some delicacy, after all, otherwise he'll tear himself to pieces and be no good to anyone.

Anyhow …

As clouds of doubt and gloom gathered over his sunny disposition, Roger continued to discuss with himself whether I was good for him or not and if the verdict came down against me, what he could do about it. He found me a constant irritant, that goes without saying, but he did have at the same time the vague suspicion that I was also the solution to his future peace and contentment and that it might be ill-advised of him to shut me up permanently, assuming that this was now even possible. Perhaps he *could* silence me, other men had surely done it; I wouldn't disappear voluntarily, though, that much was clear to him. On the positive side, he knew also that I was the incarnation of the 2+2 equation that had shaken him all those years before. If he fired me and consigned me to his past, what would happen to that?

Thanks for the mammaries, Dolly

So, dear reader, how true and meaningful you believe all that to be, and in its own way thus more or less interesting, will doubtless depend on whether you have personally ever walked down this road, or ever perceived a small, sunlit track leading into the forest of your prejudices, beliefs, lies, half-cock ideas, and ill-considered opinions; a track that you might just one day have been tempted to venture towards and explore, on the fringes of the forest, first, and then perhaps deeper and deeper into the trees … They say that most men turn quickly around and flee back to the comfort and safety of their established opinions and lives; others, it is rumoured, never return from such excursions and can be found in medical establishments of a certain variety. Either way, if you have the spirit of adventure, it's worth taking the chance, isn't it? For who knows, you may also be one of the lucky ones, the survivors, the pioneers who find the highway to a deeper sense of life which, I can promise you, dear reader, lies in that other land beyond the forest.

In the meantime, perhaps you want me to go forward in time again and return to our *story*? Yes? I thought so. One can only hold a man's attention for so long with mere thoughts!

So, where was I? I believe I left you with good old Archie trying to whitewash the attempted poisoning of the nation *for our own good* in order to be ready when the Soviets tried to do it *for real* (or, as a sceptic such as Roger might just think, in order for the government to secretly poison our own enemies if the occasion presented itself and we could get away with it).

Well, you may remember that, ever well-prepared, Roger also had a secret research report put together on Archie himself before that pleasant dinner. The following day, he called in the reporter who drafted the note to question him about it.

"This is all a bit vague," says Roger. "Don't you know any more about The Baker Biotech Institute than this? It sounds like it came off the company website."

"It did. You only gave me a day or two to do the job, so I had to confine myself to internet research."

"But what does 'biotech' even mean? Biological technology?"

"I haven't become an expert in a few hours, but in short I've grasped that its main focus is genetic engineering and cell manipulation."

"Sounds dodgy to me," says Roger. "Do you have an example of a practical application of that line of work?"

"Yes, I do, actually. A famous one. Dolly the Sheep. Remember her? I think it was our paper that got the story first. That sheep born of cloning. Genetic engineering, as I said."

"Yes, I remember. But we didn't get the clone birth story first. We got a *world exclusive* a bit later. It was well before my time, but I've still got our front-page. We revealed that the sheep was named after Dolly Parton's tits."

Charlie—that's his name—laughs heartily.

"How come?" asks the reporter, who wasn't even born, by cloning or otherwise, when all this happened.

"Mammaries. It was about mammaries. They cloned mammary glands."

"So the sheep was cloned from Dolly's tits, is that it?" the reporter ventures. He clearly enjoys trying to make his boss laugh, but fails when I tell Roger to stop being complacent with a junior and to get on with it. He has something to say first, though, it seems.

"Don't you think we're very vulgar and trivial, Charlie?" asks Roger absently.

The question quite floors the boy, who has not been accustomed to conversation in his boss's office rising above banter. He smiles awkwardly.

"As a people, I mean. Not just you and me, of course, we're obviously as vulgar as they come. 'Tits' and 'arses' and all that; that's what we do here, of course, even if we're slightly more genteel with our language in print."

Charlie understands—he's a bright lad—that he's not supposed to answer the question, and indeed Roger continues without waiting for him to do so.

"Here we have one of the discoveries, the breakthroughs, of the 20th century, perhaps of the whole of human existence —though God knows what we'll do with it, probably the worst—and our scientific community cannot think of anything better than to name its fruits after an American singer's knockers."

He pauses. I think Charlie sees that he is superfluous to the dialogue and remains silent.

"We are so vulgar," Roger insists. "We've always been a bawdy people and still are, but our problem is that we no longer know how to be serious when events or the moment merit it. If it had been a French discovery, what do you think they would have called their sheep?"

"Jean-Paul Sartre, probably," chips in Charlie. "They're all so bloody pretentious."

"I swear the French would have gone for a name that reflected some aspect of science or culture," Roger continues. "That's what they do, you know. The god 'Orisis', for example, even though he was of course a ram. In any case, they would have put a whole team of intellectuals on it, probably."

"Of course," says Charlie in a sardonic tone.

I'm so proud of my Roger today. Perhaps this young squeak isn't the right audience, but it does seem as though some of his reading and thinking is rubbing off on him.

"Let's move on," says my man. "Who was this 'Baker', anyhow, who gave his name to this research racket?"

"Well, my main focus was Samuels, of course, as you asked. He's been the director for five years or so and working in the company for twenty in all. There are a few details about his academic qualifications, but really not much more than that. And outside the Institute website, his life has left no trace at all. He's not on any social media that I can find, not even Facebook. The only thing I picked up was he got some decoration or other a few years back. Named for it by the PM, it seems. That's how it works."

"And Baker?"

"He could be more interesting, if we're digging for stuff. What's all this about, anyhow?"

"Just go on," says Roger.

"Well, Baker founded the Institute thirty years ago and then, in his fifties, about five years ago, died in *mysterious circumstances*, as they say. He was found hanging in a barn on his farm. The police said suicide, but his family didn't buy that. They started making a lot of noise after his death, hinting at the evil hand of foreign forces, or even our own guys, but then suddenly they stopped. I can't find anything more about that at all. Not a word. I did take the initiative, though, of poking around a bit more in Baker's life—this was after I wrote the report about Archie Samuels, who got Baker's job, by the way, as his deputy."

"And what did you find, if anything?"

"A lot of photos, actually. I don't know who's doing it, but someone with an apparent pseudonym has created a Facebook page in his memory. Apart from a few expressions of regret and remembrance, it just carries these photos."

"What's in them?"

"They're travel shots, as far as I can judge. With no captions or comments, but apparently taken on work trips, because there aren't any beaches, or scenery, or happy families, just Baker shaking hands and sitting at tables talking to people. A lot of Arabs with tablecloths on their heads and beards and scores of sombre-looking military men."

"Make sure you don't describe our Middle East friends like that outside this building. In any case, was there anyone you recognized?"

"Well, that's where there might be something interesting. In one photo, he's shaking hands warmly with a tall, goofy guy who I would swear is Assad, the Syrian."

"Really? That certainly wouldn't be a holiday, as you say. I wonder what he was doing with *him*."

"That's what I thought. They're the enemy, aren't they?"

"Perhaps today, perhaps not tomorrow," says Roger. "Yesterday, they were great friends. Assad even came here and met the Queen for tea, as I remember. In recent years, we've been dropping bombs on them quite a lot.

"Your next job: Drop everything else for the moment. I want you to do me a full note on Assad. I seem to remember he's gassed, or dropped chemicals, on his people, killed thousands as I recall. Get me the time-line on all that and what speculation there is about where he gets his weapons and so on. But just before you head off on that, tell me a little more about what these biotech companies and institutes are into."

"As far as I can gather," the reporter continues, "it's just a sexy way of sounding 'modern.' Even Johnson & Johnson, who make all that powder they sprinkled on our arses as children, now call themselves a 'biotech company', one of the biggest on the planet. They're into pharmaceuticals—vaccines, of course, among much else—medical devices, and all those consumer products like the bum powder."

"Did biological weapons crop up anywhere?"

"At Johnson's?"

"In any of your research on biotech outfits."

"No, they're strictly *verboten*, you know. Banned by international convention."

"Someone makes them, nevertheless."

"Sure, the usual bad guys, but they don't admit it either, of course."

"Fine, thanks Charlie, get that Assad research to me as quickly as possible, will you? The big boss is on this one, though he doesn't know it yet."

Heinrich Böll makes his entrance

I haven't spoken much about Roger's wife Sandra, have I? I do not dwell in her head too, of course, so you will understand. Practically everything interesting in people's lives goes on inside their heads and merely to describe their comings and goings and what they choose to show in external manifestations of their personalities is rarely compelling. This is perhaps why we like reading good books that take us into other minds? What otherwise do we know about the whole worlds going about their business in other human craniums? It's difficult to say, unless they talk a lot about themselves, and even then only if they blurt out their real and true thoughts, rather than a lot of well-rehearsed and repeated nonsense they want others to hear. We might observe too that it has not been the tradition in our little nation to get too personal, and certainly not demonstrably emotional, in our commerce with the others. Perhaps this is changing, though? Has already changed? If you're in the mood, you can now plunge into social media and read in great and graphic detail some fine first-hand accounts of the prostrate operations or hysterectomies of complete strangers. Do people, for all that, reveal anything authentically intimate about what's really going on inside their noddles as they live their lives, though? Could they, in fact, in the same way as the people we marry, or our friends, or close members of our own families, actually be completely unknown to us—and more often than not, perhaps even to themselves? There are certain reputable thinkers who indeed claim that we cannot know ourselves. Personally, I don't know what they are talking about. Or rather, I do. What they actually mean is that they do not know themselves and thus find it impossible, even highly distasteful, that nature might have given this opportunity to others. So, envious and resentful, they turn their own lack of such insight into a universal truth. It is something men do commonly, of course.

Whatever!

I was talking about Sandra. She seems to sense very well—the famous women's instinct, I suppose!—when Roger P. slips away from her into prolonged conversations with me. I suspect that it worries her at first, because he becomes a little distant and inscrutable, is not his otherwise cheery and garrulous self. She doesn't know (I think) about the two of us—he has been tempted to try and explain it to her but cannot yet find the way to do it without being taken for a madman or, worse, not being understood at all—and seems a bit confused when I get the upper hand and Roger's behaviour towards her changes for the better. She has even been led to believe that he is trying to "get something out" of her, as she puts it, at these times, despite his insistence that it is not the case.

Roger met Sandra far away from his newspaper world. In a bookshop, believe it or not. I had been going on at him again about his depthless ignorance and his need to read a few novels, some of the great classics, perhaps, to discover what might lie beyond 'The Daily Hack' and its crass, ersatz representations of human existence. Though he still felt as much excitement about his *scoops* and *exclusives* as when he first threw himself life and soul into the newspaper racket, he did increasingly have his moments of doubt. One of them was precisely on this day in the bookshop, which I shall recount to you ...

The sight of thousands of books gave Roger's stomach a turn. He felt quite sick. His first instinct was to turn his heels and run off to the Red Lion for a very large Scotch. But as he was contemplating instant flight, a woman emerged from an alley of shelves right in front of his nose and asked, in a tone he felt to be suspicious, "Can I help you?" To Roger, she might have said, "Do you intend to steal anything?," so guilty and confused did he feel about being in the shop in the first place.

"No, no, just looking," Roger said pathetically.

Pull yourself together, I told him, or you'll make a fool of yourself, for sure. It's only a bookshop, not a tabernacle.

Like most men who are not otherwise engaged and, being so, consciously avoid any loitering gaze upon unknown women, he sized her up. Nice looking girl, he thought. Maybe I should ask for her help, after all? She had turned and was already a few steps away when he said, "On second thoughts, perhaps you can. I didn't come in for anything in particular, but could you point me, for example, in the direction of any good novels you might have about newspapers, if such things exist."

The woman retraced her steps and said quickly, "Oh, they do, they do. A couple of classics, actually. They'll be at opposite ends of the shop, funnily enough. We organise our *great* literature in alphabetical order of authors, because most people who come in *do* know what they're looking for."

Roger took her remark and accompanying smile as malicious; I told him not to be so sensitive and to see that they were in any case actually quite becoming to her. He relaxed a little.

"The first should be right here, actually, among the 'Ws'. Wallace—David Foster, of course, the American, killed himself, poor chap. Walpole, Horace—can you imagine he wrote the first gothic novel? Here we are, Waugh, no, wrong one, son of … Evelyn, here we have it. 'Scoop', Evelyn Waugh, a wonderful little mockery about popular journalism, very funny indeed. A little racist, perhaps, as practically all writers were at the time, but keep that to yourself otherwise they'll be burning his books before you know it."

Roger already liked this woman. What knowledge! A plunge into the 'Ws' and she knew them all—he was sure she could keep going like that.

Sandra—for it was her—had been squatting to consult the book spines, and Roger took her arm in his firm grip as she pulled herself back to her feet. A strange animal current passed between them (she later confessed that she had felt it too).

"Will you take it?"

"If you recommend it, most certainly," said Roger.

"Here you are, then. Do you still want to see the other book?"

"I reckon I can handle two novels," he joked, "particularly since this one is so slim."

"So's the other. Come with me to the 'Bs'."

They walked to the far side of the shop; the 'Bs' were at

mid-height, somewhat to Roger's regret; Sandra bent her head to the left to read the book spines; he looked at her naked neck and shoulder with its light down and felt an urgent desire to kiss them, which he contained, happily.

"Here we go. Bainbridge, Beryl, horror among the working classes; Baldwin, James, black, gay, *engaged* in meaningful causes, a brilliant writer, also American, as you know." And then, stepping back half a yard to advance in the alphabet, "Boccacio, Giovanni, very naughty, sinful stories banned and burnt in their time; here we have it, Böll, Heinrich, German, of course, and bingo, we have the one for you, 'The Lost Honour of Katharina Blum,' a savage denunciation of the wretched, sensationalist, lying tabloid press and how an investigative journalist wrecks an innocent woman's life."

"Strong stuff, then," was Roger's stupid comment, though he was thinking how much he liked someone who would use a word such as 'savage' like that. And what else, my friend, I asked him? "I'll take that too," was all he could find to add.

"Very good," said Sandra. "Everybody should read *that* one. They might just then wake up and realize that we too are in the grip of such salacious, dangerous, trash media and that no one does anything about it at all. Tell me, though, why are you especially interested in novels about newspapers?"

Get out of that one, I whispered to Roger.

"Nothing in particular," he lied. "I've been thinking some of the same things as you, that's all, and wanted to see how authors handled the whole business."

Sandra smiled at this whopper and later would often remind him of the whole conversation.

A river in Egypt

Have you destroyed anyone's life, I ask Roger as he heads for the Red Lion, a book sticking jauntily out of each of his jacket pockets?

Roger barely registers my question. His thoughts are quite elsewhere. On the woman in the bookshop, in fact. Fancy that, he tells himself, I give her a vague notion of what I am supposed to be looking for, right off the top of my head, and in among hundreds and hundreds, probably thousands, of books, she swoops on two which apparently fit the bill, all the while telling me about Bainbridge, Baldwin, Walpole … What knowledge! If only she knew what I do not know, she would be shocked.

Indeed. But why do you think she cares in the slightest what you know or don't know, I ask him? I'm sure she's forgotten already even about your sorry existence.

Roger ignores me as he pushes open the doors of the Red Lion. In this matter of the attraction between men and women, instincts are of more importance than anything I might tell him, of course. In the very first instance, that is, when love remains unspoken and unquestioned and has not yet been robbed of its fragile purity by the words we then seek to inflict upon it … Have you noticed, my friends, how often men and women fall in love with someone who turns out to be completely unsuitable for them in every way? And, in the case of the most grimly persistent and lazy among them, nevertheless fumble their way through the grief of it over an entire lifetime? Of course you have. Surely you have even yourself been an unwitting victim of your misunderstandings in the matter, though you be loathe to admit it? Well, let me tell you this: It is not because we are mistaken in our initial emotions, if that's the conclusion you are jumping to. As I mentioned at the outset of this account, we feel what we feel, however absurd and inappropriate our feelings might be. It is not, either, because we are misled by some fanciful chemical reaction, much in vogue for a decade or two, by which some magical molecular potion crosses over into the spiritual sphere which is love's abode (Roger himself put an end to that myth for himself when he once fell instantly in love with a new woman informant two hundred yards away from him across a car park). As for lust, we shall not even give this animal drive one second of our present consideration of the matter. No, this mysterious love that had cast its mantle over Roger (and, we shall later discover, over Sandra too) can not be easily explained ... All we can say about it with certainty is that it is a guarantee of absolutely nothing whatsoever about whether its objects can get along with each other for five minutes even!

"I'm in love," Roger tells the tavernkeeper.

"A double, as usual, then?"

Roger nods.

The tavernkeeper stabs his little finger in his ear and shakes it violently.

"Funny, that, I thought I heard someone say he was in love. I think I'll go and have my ears checked. Aural hallucinations, they call them. An occupational hazard in my line of business. Happens when I haven't had a client for a couple of hours."

"You poor, lonely bastard," says Roger, smiling. Then, in a flash, like the saloon gunslinger of his childhood fantasies, he draws the novels from his pockets and points them at the tavernkeeper's head.

"Your money or your brain! Not that you have much of either."

Insulting his clients is the tavernkeeper's stock in trade and he takes no offense at their occasional vengeance.

"What are you doing with books, then, Roger? No one reads them any longer, do they? I've heard they all wait for the television version now." He lowers his glasses over his eyes and picks one up, declaiming, " 'Boll'? As in boll-ocks, I presume ..."

"Not, actually. 'Boell'. That's what the umlaut—those two little dots—does, my friend. 'Boell'," he says again (repeating the pronunciation lesson given by an obliging lady on the way to a cash till). "I don't think the sound exists in English, but we can do our best, can't we?"

"And this one. Evelyn *Wog*, I suppose?"

"You should rename this establishment," Roger suggests. "'The Philistine' would be a much more attractive draw than 'The Red Lion', don't you think?"

"If it were to reflect the aspirations and ambitions of my clients, that would do nicely."

"Give me another, would you?"

Roger picks up his renewed whisky and his books and goes to a table in the corner. He opens the Böll (*Boell, Boell, Boell,* he's saying to himself over and over again in the hope that he can in this way keep alive the voice of a certain woman a little longer in his besotted mind) and flicks through the pages.

I suppose I'm going to have to read you, old *Boell,* he thinks, otherwise I can't very well go back to the shop.

"Who's the unlucky girl, then?" asks the idle tavern-keeper.

"No one you'd know or would ever be likely to meet in this den of iniquity," says Roger, without looking up from the book.

Why not take this reading in a positive spirit, I suggest to Roger? Try and learn something, about events and people; stay neutral as you read; don't judge anything except the writer and whether what he's telling you is truthful, insightful, interesting, corresponds to any reality you know or can imagine, is of any importance.

Yes, boss, says Roger, I'll try. And I'll put off your question to another day, if I may—I haven't forgotten it. Have I destroyed anyone's life? You'll admit that it's a question that could get a man in serious trouble with himself if the verdict fell the wrong way. I haven't yet the strength for it, you'll admit that. Too many other, preliminary questions that I'd have to deal with before then.

It's true what the boy says. Asking yourself too many questions rarely leads to anything good, at least in the short term. Why do you think otherwise that remorse is most certainly the least-shared emotion among the perpetrators of even—what do I mean *'even'*? above all!—the most evil of crimes? Yes, of course, our societies love to parade before us the remorseful and reformed villains who are looking for or have found redemption. It's a good sales argument for Christians and all those others who have an interest in keeping the people cowering under their pulpits and benches. The truth, though, my friends, is that the repenters are actually most uncommon and count also among them a not inconsiderable number of frauds whose only remorse is about getting caught. No, men do not repent their sins, neither from honourable nor dishonourable motives. The teaching of the churches has failed miserably in this respect and left us only with the wailing of the virtuous who perhaps occasionally wish they had sins to repent. But what do criminals have to gain from remorse and repentance, particularly if they have no god upon whom they can throw themselves for mercy? Lighter sentences? This has been known. It is not, though, an accident if our prisons number more of the self-proclaimed innocent than the remorseful guilty. Indeed we find ourselves among them at this very moment. Mark Twain was right. Denial ain't just a river in Egypt.

Xenophobia at work

Roger and Sandra have a most charming new neighbour, a nice, smiling little fellow, of Southeast Asian origin, they suspect. They have speculated between them from where exactly he might hail. He only moved in a couple of weeks ago, and their encounters have not yet gone beyond nodding and smiling and, on the neighbour's part, bowing a lot, too.

Today, returning from a night shift at the newspaper, Roger sees the neighbour as he's leaving his home and suggests that they introduce themselves. The man says his name is 'Sock Sharia', as Roger understands it. Out of professional habit, he pulls out a pen and paper and asks the man to write it down. 'Sock' only laughs and says, "Have good day!," while jumping on his bicycle and riding off down the lane. Odd. Perhaps he didn't understand me, thinks Roger.

As he watches the bicycle disappearing around the bend, the post van pulls in from the opposite direction. Dan the postman, another of Roger's informants, who tips him off about the comings and goings around the houses of the many well-heeled, rather dubious personalities on his run of the rich villages and estates, hands him a pack of letters through the van window and speeds off. I think he knows that early morning is not the time to brief Roger on local gossip; he's generally in much too foul a mood after a night at the 'Hack', particularly of late.

Roger kisses Sandra, hands her the letters, and heads wordlessly up the stairs to bed. I suggest that he could make more of an effort to charm his wife when he comes home, but he ignores me, throws off his clothes and dives under the quilt.

"I'm right and you're wrong," says Sandra when he later emerges again from his sleep and comes downstairs.

"That would be a first," says Roger.

"He's from Cambodia. Not Vietnam. Or circumstantial

evidence suggests that's the case." Sandra hands him a thick envelope with several postage stamps depicting 'Kun Khmer' combatants kicking each other. "Cambodian boxing," she announces. "I looked it up."

"Sok Charya," Roger reads. "He did say his name was Sok. I met him outside this morning. Trust lazy Dan to give his mail to us. So, Cambodia, you were right, then, clever girl. I wonder how he ended up here in our leafy suburb. We'll have to find out, of course. Can't have foreigners setting up in our neighbourhood without further investigation, can we?"

"Do you have to bring your xenophobia home with you, darling? Don't you get enough of that at the office?"

Roger smiles. He doesn't share the general anti-immigrant hysteria which is one of the most solid bulwarks of the 'Hack's' editorial ideology, but it doesn't bother him much either and remains rather abstract despite my endeavours to point out to him that all the contempt spewed forth by his newspaper actually has real people on the end of it. People like Sok Charya.

"It's true, anyhow, that he's obviously not one of those impoverished refugees our bosses want to keep out of the country," says Roger. "Not living here in our affluent little village, in any case. I wonder how he came upon his means?"

"Why don't you just mind your own business, dearest?" Sandra suggests. "Anyhow, we must invite him round for lunch, or something, one of these days and I'm sure he'll tell us about it spontaneously."

"Good idea. I'll take the letter to him this evening and do just that. How about lunch on Saturday?"

"Fine—but do ask if there's anything he doesn't eat, will you? Religious reasons or whatever. I assume he's Buddhist and they are very particular about these things, really finicky. He could, of course, also be Muslim, or even Hindu, Christian at a push, even though the communists did their best to annihilate religion of any kind during the genocide. We studied all this a bit in geopolitics at university. I remember that modern Cambodia was especially complicated. And it's all a distant memory for me now, of course. It will be good to meet him and get a refresher course on all that."

Though he is as bold in his assertions as most ignorant men, Roger has long acquiesced to the evidence that Sandra is more knowledgeable than him in practically everything concerning the larger world. He, the newspaperman! When they first met, his outstanding virtuosity with bad faith, which is unequalled outside tabloid journalism, helped to get him through the worst humiliations. As he felt less and less threatened—being an eminently sensible and intelligent woman she never pressed home her advantage in discussions of either fact or opinion—he brought humour also out of his panoply of defensive weapons and often slid out of trouble on a jest and a quip. I certainly encouraged him in this direction. I've always felt that he was good material to work on, this man, and that he would not dig his heels deeper into foolishness, pretence and deception, if he saw a clear way out. For right at the heart of Roger P. is an honest and honourable man asking to be saved from himself, despite his reprehensible start in life. And as I'm sure you have grasped or are finally catching on, dear reader, it is my job to help guide him.

Autopsy of a killer

Roger and I are getting on better and better. He's feeling a lot more comfortable with me around and is actually beginning to enjoy some of our conversations. He's spending more time with me even than with some of his friends. He finds he needs them less and less—and in lucid moments suspects that they actually belong to a world he is destined one day to leave.

Let me at this juncture tell you something important that the cleverest among you may already have understood: I live in my present alone. I have no yesterdays or tomorrows to worry about, unlike Roger and, I suspect, many of you, though I don't wish to slight anyone. But, you protest, we distinctly remember you talking about your past—your origins, to be precise. You suggested that you might have been born in a kindergarten classroom during a mathematics lesson. At one moment, you seemed to be implying that you were the epiphany itself! The religious connotations did not escape us at all. So what's all this about no yesterdays, no tomorrows?

You misunderstand, my friends, it is easily done. It is not that I am *without* past or future, but that they do not concern me. When, of a cloudless morning, the sun rises in the great blue sky and warms the land and its inhabitants, it is not at all beholden to or in any way affected by the fact that it rose also yesterday and will also rise tomorrow. The sun is of this instant, always and forever.

Roger, poor chap, is condemned to drag his past around with him, of course. He has lived badly in countless ways and most certainly added to the general sum of human suffering, which is as good a measure of the worthlessness of a life as any other that leaps to mind. How can he make up for it, he asks me from time to time? Well, I don't at all encourage regret, the renouncement *a posteriori* of freely decided acts. It is not only a completely useless emotion for everyone concerned, but one that claims only that we might have acted differently had we been other than we were when we committed our misdemeanours. And that consideration, I prefer to leave to the authors of fantasies and fairy tales.

I do allow him just a little remorse, though. The capacity to say to himself, 'I was wrong and I'm sorry for the consequences.' This is how a man moves forward, ensures that if ever the same set of circumstances present themselves, he will be capable, being now another person, of acting differently than the first time.

Am I boring you, dear reader? It's true that I'm becoming a little bored myself with this autopsy of a *killer,* our nation's Public Enemy No. 1, as I suspect Roger's old colleagues will tomorrow call the man as they work themselves into a frenzy at the astonishing opportunity that the gods of newspapers have provided by the fact that this by-then fugitive was *theirs* and that nothing the competitors will ever be able to dream up can ever take away the advantage that this gives the 'The Daily Hack'. Our very own Pretty Boy Floyd was just yesterday sitting innocently in the newsroom, drinking tea and chatting amiably with the cleaning ladies. Little did we know …

You yearn for more of our *story,* but you must understand that I am giving you an almost unique opportunity to grasp the nature of a man *from the inside.* How often do you get a break like that? Normally, of course, you wouldn't care very much at all to learn about everything that goes on in a man's head. But when he is a *convicted double killer,* all that changes, doesn't it? Then, you simply can't get enough, can you?

The French film-maker Jean-Luc Godard, who died just the other day, said that all stories should have a beginning, a middle, and an end, 'but not necessarily in that order.' I agree with him, and could right now go back or forward. I think I'll advance; we have plenty of time—quite literally a lifetime, if Roger's evasion plan fails—to circle round and return to earlier days again.

Suspicious behaviour

So, you are asking yourself: What did that Sok fellow have to do with anything? Perhaps you did not attentively read the *full story* of Roger P.'s heinous crime in the newspapers, or you would know. But anyhow.

Sok Charya has a dog. It seems to like Roger and Sandra. In fact, in common with many dogs, it likes everyone, whether they reciprocate its affection or not. Roger does not. Indeed, he cannot abide dogs at all. When Sok is out of earshot, Roger curses this animal and, though he would like to kick it, restrains himself and merely hisses, "cur, swine, I hate you," and other niceties as the dog salivates around his ankles.

This evening, as planned, Roger goes next door to give Sok his letter. No one answers the doorbell, so he slips round the side alley to the garden gate and shouts "Hello." Sok soon appears, bowing deeply and smiling broadly as usual when he sees Roger.

"I read your newspaper!" Sok announces proudly, flapping 'The Daily Hack' in Roger's face. "Improve English. Nice see you."

Roger gives him the letter, all the while keeping an eye on the rest of the garden to make sure the dog doesn't suddenly emerge and bound towards him. He sees, though, that it is playing alone with a large bone, and that the idea of throwing itself with love on Roger has apparently not yet crossed its mind.

Sok stops smiling when he looks at the envelope Roger is holding out to him. He takes it, then rather gauchely drops his hand and dissimulates it behind his back.

"From home?" Roger asks impudently.

"*This* my home," says Sok.

He looks irritated, Roger, I tell him. Drop it for now. Roger obliges, and asks Sok whether he would like to come over for lunch the following Saturday. Sok nods diffidently, apparently still preoccupied by his envelope, and only says "Yes, please."

"If you'd like to bring someone with you, they'd be most welcome too," Roger adds.

"No, no. Only Fred," he says, pointing back over his shoulder at his dog.

"You'll be alone, then," Roger asserts, to rule out the dreadful prospect of a dog in his dining room.

They fix the time and Roger only adds: "Sandra—my wife—wants to know if there is anything you prefer not to eat. Is there?"

"No, no, eat anything."

"Right, then. See you Saturday latest," Roger concludes as he shuts the garden gate behind him and goes home.

"So, will he come? Was he pleased to get his letter?"

"Yes, he accepted the invitation. He behaved in the strangest of ways about the letter, though. Practically hid it behind his back, which is rather stupid. He was just boasting that he read my newspaper, but then clamped up completely and began to twitch nervously when I handed him the envelope. There's something odd about it all."

"Well, Mister Investigations Editor will just have to get it out of him on Saturday, won't he?"

"I'm looking forward to it suddenly," says Roger.

A cup of tea with the Queen

"So, old Bashar? How long has he been gassing his people and where does he get the goods?"

Charlie sits down at Roger's desk and pulls out his notepad.

"Right. He seems to have begun the nasty little business of bombing his folks with sarin eight or nine years ago, in a suburb of Damascus itself, and hasn't looked back, with dozens of chemical attacks in the following five years."

"You said sarin?"

"Yep. Chlorine and sulphur mustard too, according to the various commissions of inquiry. Hundreds, perhaps thousands, killed and poisoned."

"All this well after his tea with the Queen, then?"

"Sure. At that time, he was just a nasty little nepotistic dictator eliminating his real or imagined opponents in one way or another. We have no problem with those kinds of leaders; they're always welcome, particularly if we can get something out of them. Why we dragged the Queen into it, I don't know. You'd think we would have kept the most abject specimens away from *her*, at least."

"Quite," says Roger.

"Anyhow, you asked me to find out where Assad gets his chemical weapons. He produces his own, apparently, and had amassed a huge stockpile of sarin, mustard gas, VX nerve agent and other such stuff—all of it actually *declared*, believe it or not—by the time he got round to signing the convention that bans all that and obliges its signatories to destroy their stocks. No one appears to have completed *that* job, not the US, UK or anyone else that I could find. And they started way back in the late nineties."

"And what do you conclude from that?" asks Roger.

"I would imagine most countries are dragging their feet and holding on to some for *special occasions*, as it were."

"So Syria could be using old stuff, too?"

"Sure. Or maybe they're still making it, who knows? Who trusts such rogue states—even our own boys, to be honest—to respect such international agreements, anyhow? That's a bit of a farce if you ask me."

"Is that all?" asks Roger.

"One other thing. Various intelligence sources suggest

that some Western European—and US—businesses who specialize in this pretty trade have been helping Assad and others to continue chemical weapon production through a nebulous network of front companies. We don't know who they are, of course, though someone must."

"So we're not any closer to finding out why Baker met Assad."

"No," says Charlie. "But I did at least get our IT boys to *date* the photo and thus the meeting. It took place the year before his first mass gas attack."

"And Baker's death, when *exactly* was that, again?"

"Three months after the attack."

"I think we need to track down and talk to Baker's family. About why they protested about the suicide verdict and then clamped up."

"Just what I was thinking, boss; I'm onto it."

"Stop calling me boss will you Charlie," Roger orders as the young reporter dashes off.

The beef goes down badly

"A pious and blessed man," says Sandra, who is arranging plates on the table as Roger opens a wine bottle.

"What?" says Roger, "I assume that you're not talking about *me*."

"That's what Charya means; it's his given name, of course, they do it backwards from us."

"How do you know that?"

"I looked it up, of course. You can't live with an Investigations Editor without some of his modus operandi rubbing off on you."

Roger laughs. "Bravo, in any case. My boys didn't even

think about doing that for me."

"What do you mean? You didn't really have him investigated, did you? I thought you were joking."

"Just a few inquiries about how a wealthy old Cambodian might enter this country to live."

"And?"

"Well, it seems that despite all the government's anti-immigration policies and pronouncements, just about anyone can find a way anyhow if he's got enough dosh. The original scheme was dropped recently, but our friend obviously got in before that happened or found some other way. Maybe it was because he was not only rich, but pious and blessed too."

Sandra smiles. "Anyhow, it quite suits him from what I've seen, don't you think?"

"I'm not sensitive to such things," says Roger, with some truth.

The doorbell rings and Roger welcomes Sok Charya. There's much bowing and scraping in which both Roger and Sandra also indulge, even doing it to each other. Don't be a smart alec, Roger, I advise him. He can be so childish at times!

"Thank your invitation, Misses," says Sok as they sit down to lunch.

Sandra laughs. "Let's not be formal. I'm Sandra."

"And I'm Roger."

Sok smiles and says nothing.

Roger and Sandra look at each other and, after an awkward silence, Roger says: "And you? What do you prefer we call you?" Roger smartly doesn't let on that they've noted his name from the envelope.

"I Sok Charya. I like you call me 'Sok'."

"Well, that's settled, then," says Roger. "Let's eat; I'm starving."

Sok says nothing as he picks a little at his food. Not a great eater, thinks Roger, who doesn't really trust anybody who doesn't have a good appetite. Let's see if he's a conversationalist, at least, he says to himself.

I see no cause for my own intervention at this stage, and keep quiet.

"Tell us a little about yourself," Sandra says, before Roger can get himself into interrogation mode. "If you'd like to, of course! We don't want to be indiscreet, do we Roger?"

"No, of course not," says Roger, with a chilling lack of conviction.

Make an effort, man, I urge him. It's clear to me that for some unfathomable reason, Roger is quickly taking a dislike to their guest. Instinct, they say, and over that I have no influence at all.

Sok is very slowly, interminably, grinding down a mouthful of beef (I'm sure that Sandra has noticed and is torturing herself about whether he got a tough piece, however fine their own are) and apparently now sets about chewing with some difficulty her question too.

After an uneasy minute or two of silence and the final passage of the beef into his intestines, Sok says: "I from Cambodia."

"Really?" says Sandra. "How *interesting*." She looks at Roger as though pleading that he make an effort to look *interested* too. But Roger is now on a mission and asks a little bluntly, "How long have you been in our country? Why did you leave home, assuming that's where you came from?"

Sok has quickly slipped another chunk of steak into his face during the question and points with his fork at his mouth to signify that he is temporarily unable to answer. When, five minutes later, with Sandra now visibly distressed about her cooking, the last piece goes down Sok's gullet, he finally replies.

"My home *here*. Left Cambodia many years ago. Made many money in business there. Come here for retire."

Is that it, Roger thinks? It seems so.

Hasn't picked up much of the lingo has he, in all these years, I observe?

Good point, Roger commends me.

What now, supersnoop, I ask him?

"So, you lived elsewhere here before coming to our little village?" Sandra asks.

"Many places. I like move. See your beautiful country."

Doesn't much sound like the life of a retiree, does it, son, I remark to Roger.

"And Cambodia? You've had a pretty rough time there over the years, haven't you? What did you do during the genocide?" The boy goes straight for the jugular, you can't fault him on that.

"Long time ago. Bad times. Me poor peasant then. Don't like speak."

Sok bows his head, gives them both a distressed look, and lays down his knife and fork firmly on his plate as if to signify he is not inclined to go on with either the conversation or the lunch.

Roger looks at Sandra in the hope that she will rescue them. She knows her man and does as his eyes request of her.

"Yes, Sok, we understand. Those times must have been terrible for you and your family. We won't talk about it any longer. Would you like some more beef?"

As Sok shakes his head slowly to decline, there's a faint bump on the front door and something that sounds like a scratch. Roger goes to see and opens the door to a friendly Labrador with a huge bone in its mouth. "Fuck off, you mongrel," Roger suggests quietly, giving the dog a gentle push with his foot. The dog doesn't seem to want to argue, turns, and runs off back to Sok's house.

"It was Fred."

"Fred?" asks Sandra. "Who's that? Not your *editor*?"

"My dog," says Sok brightly, finally smiling again.

"He didn't seem to want to come in, I'm afraid," lies

Roger. "Perhaps just wanted to check that you were still here. Anyhow, he seems quite happy alone with his bone."

"Bone?" asks a puzzled-looking Sok. "He have no bone."

"Oh yes he does," says Roger. "A very big one too. Looks like he finally got hold of the man's leg he's been after."

Sok frowns. He is not amused, I tell Roger.

Sandra invites them to go to the sitting room where she'll bring some dessert, if Roger will pour the coffee.

Sok gets up, wipes his mouth, and, in short, makes his excuses. Says he must go and check Fred and, in any case, is very tired. "I old man," he says weakly. "Need bed!"

"Well, that was a comprehensive disaster," says Sandra, when Sok has gone. He had been with them for less than an hour and they had managed to upset him. "Could you not have been a little more delicate than to throw in the genocide in the middle of the lunch?"

She's right, of course, but as I've said, once Roger cuts himself loose on a grilling, no man is safe. There's very little that I can do about it, frankly.

"Something's not right about the man," says Roger. "I can almost smell it. I need to know a bit more about old Sok, how he came to get his money, and why he's moving around the country like that when he's supposed to be enjoying his retirement. And why his English is still so lousy after all these years."

"No neighbour is safe with you around," jokes Sandra. "Can you handle two investigations at once? First Archie, now Sok. Are there others? How about that ostentatious Russian up the road, Lev isn't it? I reckon he should be your priority."

"He's taken care of already," Roger confesses. "We know all about him, but he's friends with people in high places, including our owner, actually, and probably with the PM too. He's off bounds."

"It's disgusting, outrageous, but I'm happy that you are honest with me, darling," says Sandra. "I can't really comprehend why I love a man engaged in such an abject, compromising business, but I do."

"Perhaps you see the promise in me," Roger suggests. The boy is getting smarter by the day. That was clever and likely true.

Having cleaned up and both feeling tired, they decide also to turn in for a siesta. Lying quietly in bed, both reading books, Sandra suddenly asks: "I've never asked you before, but did you have *me* investigated before we got seriously *involved*, as the expression goes?"

"Just a few background checks and a couple of briefing notes from the team."

Sandra smashes a pillow in Roger's face and only just hears his answer and laughter as she attempts to smother him. "I'm joking!"

Love will never change the world

Since we're on the subject, how *did* Roger win over Sandra's heart after that first meeting in the bookshop?

He had gone home from the newly-renamed 'Philistine' when a rowdy gang of its regular zealots had arrived braying loudly about their desire to get *completely slaughtered*. It was clearly not the best environment to get acquainted with Herr Böll's work.

Now one of the highest paid reporters on the 'Hack', well rewarded for a series of exclusive articles on the secret lovers of a number of the country's leading film actors and actresses, a huge sales boost, Roger lived in a handsome mews house on a hidden cobbled street. Inside, it was a shambles, because our man didn't care in the slightest about good order and appearances (Sandra has long ago put him right about these matters). When he thought he might bring girls home, he superficially straightened things out, but he didn't give them much time to study their surroundings, having other matters in mind than idle conversation.

As extraordinary as this may sound to you, dear reader, he had no bookshelves nor books! One hears that this has become common in the homes of the nation. If confronted by a cultivated man about this aberration, the bookless will claim that it's a waste of space but that they do, of course, read still, though on electronic devices, or failing that, that they listen to books while driving to work. Perhaps it is so, indeed.

So, Roger sits down upon reaching home and starts reading his *Boell*. If you are hoping that it will be a revelation to him, my friends, I may have to disappoint you. If a single book could fundamentally change a man, the social services would be handing out the most thoughtful of them on street corners. We do know that they can irritate, even anger, a reader, though, particularly when they challenge his prejudices and misconceptions and, of course, his beliefs. People do not on the whole read books to disturb their peace of mind, to rattle themselves, which is why so many successful novels today have nothing at all to do with the lives that people actually live. What a good book just might do, if the exasperated, vexed reader hasn't prematurely chucked it on the fire, is to plant a few questions in his mind. For this to happen, he must of course be open to it, ready to challenge himself, examine why it's getting on his nerves. Happily, Roger today is in such a mood, not—I must be modest—because of my now unceasing efforts to wrench his mind away from its usual bearings, but simply because he is in love, or thinks he is, which, all feelings being by their nature authentic, as I have said, comes to exactly the same thing. To be in love is to open wide your mind to the thoughts and beliefs of the other. And the lady in the bookshop, the object of his swooning soul, has passionately advised him that *Boell* is essential reading to *wake him up*. She hadn't said *him*, of course, but *everyone*, which was pretty much the same thing, when all is said and done.

Love thus became my ally, which is quite remarkable, and quite beautiful really.

But weren't you precisely denigrating those people, pop singers and the rest, the churches, probably the Pope in person, who implore us to love each other and in doing so change the world? We've caught you out there. You're confused or a hypocrite! But no, ladies and gentlemen, I regret that you are wrong in this instance. My objective is not to speak against love! My point is that you cannot command it and that you are wasting your breath in trying to do so. I sometimes even suspect that there is only a given, fixed amount to go around and that as new people begin to love, others give up and decide it's easier and more rewarding to hate! Be that as it may, you cannot will it, nor can you order it on the internet. Good Lord, people can go for years, perhaps their whole lives, looking for love that they never find. So what I am saying is that we cannot wait, especially since we have no particular reason to think things in this regard will change any time soon. Did you see those love-preaching Buddhist monks in Myanmar who've been leading the slaughter, the genocide, of their Muslim neighbours in the thousands? Or good old Patriarch Kirill of Moscow urging the Kremlin to wipe out Ukraine and his coreligionists there? Religion no more inspires love than does football. Even less, probably, now I think about it. It's an abstraction, a pretence, this idea that love learned from preaching will change anything at all on a grand scale. Indeed, it's even worse than we can possibly imagine. History has shown us that the worst torturers and butchers do love their wives and children and dogs, and quite possibly their neighbours, as much as anyone else. A man who loves does not do so because he hangs his coat on the clothes pegs of churches, mosques or temples. You do not even need to love yourself nor your neighbour to be a good man! To believe so is one of the great foolishnesses of the recent history of our species. If there is a man who in his mind loves reason, truth and justice, however—well, now we are talking!

Pax in ignorantia

She didn't tell me *that*, Roger says to himself. He's been surprised to find that Katharina, the tabloid victim, has shot and killed the journalist investigating her.

The spirit in which he is reading this book is not at all the right one, is not at all what I have been trying to teach him. Is it really so difficult for a man like Roger, any man, come to that, to free his mind of its habitual word clutter in order to come at an argument, a tale, an essay, whatever, without constantly judging it in the light of his own preconceptions? Yes, apparently, it is very difficult indeed. From our personal experience and from what we observe in others, that is. Roger's first instinct, of course, is to dismiss even the prospect that this radical leftist German author could have a clue about his own business, profession and the tabloid culture. Perhaps we are all inclined to look for fault when outsiders meddle in the stuff of our lives and identities? This misguided instinct today even has its own appellation, *cultural appropriation,* used to dismiss out of hand the expression of anything by anyone other than he who is in question. I remind Roger that he had himself led the charge in the latest 'Daily Hack' assault on the so-called *woke* ideology, when he had actually used his whole panoply of dismissive contempt against this idea that he was now employing against his own brief enemy, Herr Heinrich Böll. Roger just snorts, not one of his most attractive habits.

Roger would have already tossed this ignorant, fanciful indictment of his brand of journalism out of the window if he had been able for a moment to forget why he was reading it in the first place. She thought highly of it; the journalist had *wrecked an innocent woman's life,* if he remembered her words correctly, and that was not something to be laughed off, taken lightly; she had described the tabloids as *wretched* and *lying,* yes he was certain about those words.

Dear me, Roger, that puts you in a bit of a pickle with the dame, doesn't it? Consider your options: You can go back to the shop, tell her the book is a load of old cobblers and not at all like reality, and bluff it out. Roger thinks that this is the best, most promising course of action. Maybe she'll appreciate me defending my job, he thinks. I suggest gently that she is perhaps not especially inflicted with the Stockholm syndrome and will rather more be inclined to kick him into the street.

No, Roger, I propose, take this challenge otherwise. I know you barely have the strength for it, but here's what I think you should do. Why don't you, as an experiment, for once just clear your mind of the past and the present and let our Mister *Boell* tell his story on a blank page, remaining cool and lucid and dispassionate and non-judgemental until he has done so and you can think about it and give the lady a balanced and unbiased opinion on its merits.

And you, he asks me? Will you keep quiet, remain absolutely silent, until I'm through with it?

Mum's the word, I tell him.

Doing his best to get absorbed in the story, and killing in the bud his temptations to defend the police and the press —and himself—in their will to pin a crime on the innocent Katharina Blum, before she actually does commit the irreparable, that is, Roger's thoughts inevitably keep turning away to himself and the morning's question: Has *he* destroyed anyone's life?

Like surgeons who inevitably kill the odd patient or two during their careers, Roger has never allowed himself to dwell on the fate of the people who get on the wrong end of one of his team's investigations. This has been less of a deliberate choice, than his natural inclination and ability always to *move on* with his life rather than to chew over what's done and finished. If you can manage it, if you are not especially a man, for example, who likes to consider the consequences of his acts, it's certainly the best way to remain at peace with yourself. *Pax in ignorantia,* my friends.

When he actually made the effort, though, Roger could remember a lot of things to which he had never given any subsequent thought at all once they were behind him. I should explain that as a merchant of stories, Roger slices up the whole of his existence in their terms. This or that month saw his famous exposé of the game show cheating scandal; another was chalked off as the downfall of a politician Roger had entrapped in a prostitution ring. October of the previous year, for example, had been the month of his scoop about the paedophile wrestling coach and the most unorthodox holds he had been practising on his young prodigies. Roger had heard the rumours through a friend of a friend and had relentlessly tracked down the pervert's victims and made them talk despite the fact that many of them were trying to forget their trauma. On the basis of the accounts he had managed to wring out of them, mostly with the argument that the man should be punished and put forever out of the reach of children and that this could not be done without their accusations, the coach had been charged and eventually sent to prison, where he hung himself before his trial.

Is that what you're looking for, Roger asks me?

I'm not looking for anything, I tell him. It's you who must hold yourself to account, if you want to do so. I'm just here to encourage you.

Well, I'm certainly not going to feel guilty about that one, says Roger. Apart from the victims, who said they would have liked an opportunity to confront him, the 'Hack' and I were applauded and thanked by our readers, who would of course have liked him to have been castrated and beheaded, but we can't arrange such things. What more could you ask?

I'm not sure that the readers of the 'Hack' are exactly a reliable gauge about questions of appropriate punishment and certainly not about ethics and morality, I tell Roger. You should be making such judgements uniquely for yourself.

Roger was tired of such questions and invited me to shut up, to go away. I knew I would talk to him later when he found the courage to go back to the bookshop. In the meantime, he had a second novel to read, which turned out to be nothing but pleasure. Waugh made a farce of the whole journalism business, ridiculed everyone, but accused no one. Roger's conscience, if we can call it that, eased through 'Scoop' and even made him feel good about himself, which I'm not sure is such a good thing at this stage in his development. No, not good at all.

Our man in Phnom Penh

"So, what have you got on my Cambodian?" The task of investigating his new neighbour has fallen to another young, eager member of his team, Marjorie.

"I followed his tracks back to three of his former addresses, one in the North East, another in the South West, and a third one back up in the North, but the trail ran out there, according to the records I could turn up. He spent no more than a year or two in any one of these places."

"And do you know when exactly it was that he came to this country, before moving around like that?"

"Yes, though not before greasing a palm or two," says

Marjorie. "You'll see it on my expenses. Not cheap."

"And?"

"Fifteen years ago. Came in under some special government scheme. His file says nothing, though. If there were background checks—as there are supposed to be—none of the results ended up in his dossier. It's all extremely vague."

Roger makes a mental note to have the system checked out when they don't have much else to turn into a scandal. He has the headline already, like any good tabloid reporter setting off to find a story: *We Don't Even Know Who They Are!* With a strapline on *Shocking New Immigration Infamy*. Or somesuch. Yes, it would make a decent piece.

"So, what do you propose? How can we get more?" asks Roger.

"Do we have a bureau in Phnom Penh?"

"What century are you living in, Marjorie? You must be kidding. We can hardly cover the distant reaches of our own country these days, let alone such far-flung places. Our readers don't give a shit what's happening in the world anyhow, unless it affects them directly, which it never does. Or rather it may do, but they are too stupid to grasp that and it's not our job to convince them. Give 'em what they want, not what they need. We're quacks, not doctors. That's our religion, isn't it?"

Careful, Roger, I advise him. Don't go showing your new existential insecurities to your colleagues. Nothing good can possibly come from it.

They remain silent for a minute or two, then Roger suggests: "This is one for the private sector, I think. We can't put an agency on it, because we want to keep things to ourselves. Find some investigator out there, will you, and get him to make the background checks on Sok that our immigration bureaucrats apparently couldn't be arsed to do."

"It'll be very expensive, you know."

"I know. But I have a hunch we're on to something. Nothing looks clean about this guy's story. And have a look at the

Cambodian networks here at home while you're at it. There are bound to be a few, as always. Some regime-friendly, others against. It's a communist dictatorship posing as a constitutional monarchy, as you are fully aware."

Marjorie smiles at the boss's irony. I don't think that last week she even knew that Cambodia existed.

Killing the uneducated

Illum oportet crescere me autem minui. He must become greater; I must become less. Do you know who said that, dear reader? John the Baptist, talking with commendable modesty about himself and Christ, of course. I do not take myself as a saint, nor the messiah, do not fear! But the ambition applies well to our little case too, is really quite apt when you think about it.

As a start, I could become less intrusive, couldn't I? Roger cannot walk around for ever being chastised and cross-examined at every step, after all, and that's something that has become a danger since he allowed that my voice should be heard, accepted to give me a rôle in his life. As I've suggested before, he could have tried to eliminate me completely. In short, we must give the man credit that he is willing to share his mind with me.

One day when he was feeling strong and happy, those fragile and often elusive states that can come and go with no rhyme nor reason, he decided to lay things out for himself, to take stock, if you like.

He has not yet dared to go back to the bookshop to begin his courtship of the lady there, because he doesn't feel that he has the answers to any of the questions that she might ask of him. Not why he does what he does for a living, nor who he really might be. (He can hardly mention me, can he? The lady would be in her rights to flee at great haste if he did that!). He senses that one cannot begin an authentic story (as opposed to his usual dalliances) with a woman on false premises, and this rather more as a practical than a moral principle; that to deceive and dissimulate at the outset will be to sow the seeds of defeat; that there is no going back if the foundations of love are built on lies. That he even contemplates these dreary thoughts, which could have come straight off the 'Hack's' agony aunt pages, shows clearly that this woman—his future wife—is not in his mind like any other with whom he has become entangled. Messily so, in most of those other cases. He knows he's thinking about the matter in clichés, but esteems that they are true nevertheless. There are a lot of women, he thinks, who have a deep loathing of deliberate falsehood. She might just be one of them. The clever chap has figured all this out for himself, because it is largely instinctive.

I would have much preferred that you had come to these conclusions on the grounds of something a little more righteous and noble than because you think lying might repulse her, scare her off, I tell him. But either way, you have quite a task, Roger old son. Here you are, a trader in cock and bull stories not only undissimulated but destined for eternity to go round and round on the internet for all the voyeurs in the land to relish at their leisure, faced with having to convince an honourable lady that you are worth the time of day.

Where on earth do I begin, asks Roger miserably?

Perhaps you could explain that you didn't actually have an adolescence, I suggest, and that this may be at the root of your complete failure to develop any maturity or values in the matter of human affairs.

Adolescents don't sit around debating morality and ethics, he counters. They're stuck into video games, or gory movies, or experimenting with any illicit substance that they can lay their hands on. At least where he comes from, the labouring classes. A fringe, of course, stay at home dreaming of how to save or to destroy the world, but they are really a minority.

But perhaps you are special, my son, I propose?

In what way, he asks? I think I'm a perfectly ordinary bloke, actually, who got a wonderful chance to realize a kid's dream of fame and fortune while having a ball of a time. And then you slowly but surely insinuate yourself into my life and try and persuade me that I'm an ignorant louse who needs to seriously reform himself to become a decent human being.

I pursue my line of questioning: So, you believe that you are, as you say, ordinary, commonplace, just a regular guy? You think, then, that everybody faces these same trials through which I am putting you?

Roger pauses to think. Perhaps yes, he says finally. After all, no one can see what I'm going through, nobody has the first clue about it, actually, so why couldn't it be true of all the others too?

Not a bad answer, I think, before adding: Where do their stories end then?

They probably knock themselves off if they feel anything like I do, he says.

We both laugh.

No, dear Roger, they don't, or the country would have become completely depopulated by now, so many *ordinary* people like you are there everywhere you look. Let me speculate a few moments. Let's suppose for an instant—it could be true, after all—that everyone indeed lives with his or her spectator (if you will allow me to continue to benevolently describe myself thus). It's true what you say, of course—we are not inside anyone else's head, so can only do our best to guess what, if anything, is going on there from what they tell us or what we can observe from the outside. Well, though it's impossible to refute that some people are clearly living on rudderless rafts cascading along mental streams of consciousness, there are also a lot of thoughtful people about too, who do take time out from these rushing word rivers to sit back and think about what they are thinking about and why they are thinking it. Self-awareness, they usually call it. Well, these people (according to research, as you may remember from that article you read in one of the serious papers you peruse) constitute only a minority of our species still, but they are here among us, this is so. In my view, though, we can go even further and subdivide the self-aware. There are, first of all, those who see clearly that they are uninteresting and worthless and often dishonest and deceitful to boot. And what do these people generally do about it, apart from wallowing in self-pity on Twitter? Nothing at all. They do their best to forget that they ever became aware of this state of affairs, suspend any further consideration of the matter, and plunge into the maelstrom of pleasures and forgetfulness available to most men and women in our society. If they didn't, it would be difficult for them to go on living. Most of them watch an excessive number of television series and movies and then buy your 'Hack' to read about them all over again. Then there is the second type of self-aware person who, catching glimpses of his mediocrity, decides to do something about it, sometimes because he believes that this will make him happier, in other cases—perhaps, Roger, you are an example?—because he seems to have no choice in the matter; that he has an inner compulsion to become a better human being in the eyes of his spectator. I simplify things, I know, and there are obviously all sorts of variations among the aware, that goes without saying. But you get the point.

Why me, though, why me, asks Roger forlornly? Why couldn't I just overlook that I'm basically a worthless shit and drown in a *maelstrom of pleasures,* as you so enticingly describe this attractive fate?

Because of two things probably, I tell him. In the first place, because you are a man of *passion,* unable to do things by half measure, condemned to pursue the goal on which you have set your sights until you reach it or, alternatively, meet a brick wall, upon which you will change direction and charge off in pursuit of some other unholy grail. It is your misfortune, of course, to have fallen while a mere embryo of a human being into the vile world of tabloid reporting and, finding yourself there, practically by accident, that you desired with all your heart to become a star on its stage. All things considered, we should count ourselves lucky that it was not, after all, a career as serial killer that attracted you, though I shouldn't mention that to the lady, if I were you, it might be misconstrued.

And my other distinguishing feature, he asks? The other card in my pack as the model seducer?

Haha! I like that Roger, I tell him. You are becoming quite ironic, old man. Well, you could claim, because it's true, that aside from this passionate nature that led you to dive unthinkingly into the swamps of Hades, you have me (though you must be very careful how you put this to her. I would simply use a common term such as *conscience*, if I were you).

And a lot of good that has brought me, Roger mutters to himself.

Come, come, my dear boy, cheer up! You'll see in the end that you are actually quite lucky in this. For a start, I believe it will get you your Dulcinea; or at least give you a chance, because without me your prospects are absolutely zero.

Maybe so, thinks Roger. But who are you, anyhow? We've never really addressed that question, have we? Who am I dealing with? And why are you there, aside from your apparent ambition to make my life a complete misery?

At this point, dear reader, I would like to ask you a very personal question, if you will permit it. Do you have your own spectator? Think about it. Perhaps a little pipsqueak timidly hinting that you are full of nonsense, like most people, and know nothing? Or, indeed, a thundering voice of reprobation that's making it difficult for you to get through your days with any peace of mind and happiness at all? If this character is nowhere to be seen in the theatre of your mind, if, in other words, you really don't know what I'm talking about, then you will probably have abandoned my story already, unable as you are to *relate* to it, which seems to be a requirement of readers in our age, who appear less and less inclined to go beyond themselves in any meaningful way. In short, they desire to read about people like themselves and, failing that, characters—perhaps aliens?—so remote from them that they do not touch at all upon their actual lives. And who am I to say that's a bad thing?

In any case, I am more optimistic by the day about this whole question as I observe the number of people, mostly Americans for the moment (our self-obsessed friends over there continue to lead the world in the identification of human foibles and mental infirmities real and imagined) who are *coming out*, as the expression goes, as sufferers of the so-called 'Impostor Syndrome'. I hope you will agree that this is hugely encouraging, my friends, since I cannot conceive that one might experience such a state of mind if one did not indeed have one's inner observer, judge, critic, voice, spectator, or whatever you are inclined to call our distinguished guild. The really funny thing, though, is that to declare yourself as a sufferer of 'Impostor Syndrome' is to deviously imply that you are, in fact, really quite outstanding at what you do, but incomprehensibly afflicted by doubt about it, as indeed we all should be if we are to become decent Socratic material. The error of the self-outed Syndrome sufferers, as they make their public bids to be lauded for modesty and self-criticism, is that they fail to see that they really are frauds and that it's only the indecent haste of the others to re-anoint them as wonderful and talented that prevents them from accepting it. To say, "I suffer from Impostor Syndrome" is in essence to betray yourself and hand the verdict on your abilities back to the mob, though they most likely will reconfirm your genius, otherwise you wouldn't have taken the risk, would you? We don't want anyone saying, "He's right! An impostor! He really cannot do his job, is a lousy actor, a crappy speaker, generally incompetent," after all. Do we?

Anyhow, where was I? Roger, do you remember those background articles about serial killers you wrote when we had one of our very own, home-grown specimens? Do you recall what stuck in your mind about one of the most famous —Ted Bundy, an intelligent and charismatic chap, like you really, who murdered upwards of thirty-five women? It was his confession to shrinks that when he went in search of his next victim he needed to be extremely drunk in order *to sedate the dominant personality who might prevent him from acting on his impulses*. Interesting, no? Can you see the parallel? You, of course, thank heaven on high, do not have that man's dreadful, perverse desires. But you too do sedate me with whisky in order to get me out of the way, don't you? And you are capable of some very naughty things when this happens, aren't you? If nothing easily classifiable as criminal, it goes without saying. So what shall we indeed call that obstructive intruder within Bundy, or you, for that matter, who needs to be taken out of the picture in order for you both to assuage your impulses and desires. The tried and tested old conscience? Why not? No one can quite agree on what that might be, but you will remember from our first readings in philosophy that Socrates nicely identified it as the *inner voice* which speaks up when we are about to make a mistake. As time has passed, of course, this censorious rôle, which Socrates wrested permanently from the gods (though he could not express it thus or did not fully understand that it was this that had happened) has greatly expanded and developed and gone well beyond such a limited ambition as that of a mere preventor of blunders. Hence, yours truly!

I agree, says Roger. *You* cannot keep quiet on a pretty much permanent basis. You are with me practically all the time, whether I'm making mistakes or only innocently going about my daily business.

Socrates was right though, as I'm sure you will also concur, Roger, when he suggested that this conscience, this arbiter of right and wrong, was born of *learning*. He could not have meant lessons in morality, surely? Or 'values', or even ethics. No one ever became a good man because he was instructed in these matters, did he? No, Roger, he was certainly talking about learning that 2+2 equals 4 and everything that grows out of *that*.

Not that again, Roger protests. You're becoming a real bore about that. Everyone accepts that 2+2 equals 4, but we don't see less strife and conflict in the world for all that.

Quite so. And do you know why? It is because they have no one to remind them of it, like you do me, no conscience, if you want, no inner voice, for sure, no spectator watching their every move, in short. The equation has been lost in the deep, dark past of their childhoods, swept into the cobwebbed recesses of their minds. They have never built anything at all on its foundations, not reason, nor truth, nor a personal doctrine of justice. In the conduct of their lives, they rush to constant judgement and action on a great tide of emotion and instinct and prejudice and nothing can hold them back. They would rather slit your throat without questions than turn honestly upon themselves and ask why it is that they permit themselves to kill you, without any examination of what they actually know of you personally, without proof that you are responsible for anything reprehensible, without any rational grounds for their actions at all. The ease with which they can commit the most abject crimes, these unthinking swine, is breathtaking. We see it every day right now, in Ukraine, as young men are called from the loving, warm hearths of their grandmothers in the remote villages of, let's say, Siberia, given a uniform and gun, and within days or weeks are raping, torturing, executing, shooting their way through their neighbour's lands. And do not think for a moment, Roger, that this would be very different with the armies of X, Y or Z nation. These are men who have nothing at all between their instincts and their actions, no inner voice, no spectator, to hold them back and ask them what they are doing and why they are doing it. And they are everywhere and in every epoch and there are legions of them.

Everyone says it's a lack of education, Roger proposes meekly.

Savages, all of them, that's what we try and tell ourselves, isn't it? But has it ever occurred to you, my boy, to think about who it is who's designing and manufacturing the guns, the missiles, the fighter jets, the thermobarbic bombs, the cluster munitions, the fléchettes, the laser cannons, the drones, the tanks, the artillery, the rocket-borne chemical agents which are massacring and mutilating thousands of people somewhere or other on any given day? The uneducated, perhaps? No, my lad, these highly sophisticated weapons of war are being conceived and produced and 'delivered', by nice boys and girls who went to Harvard and Cambridge and the Polytechnique, who by day dream up even more efficient and cruel and painful ways to kill their fellow human beings and go home to their comfy homes and families in the evenings with totally free minds and hearts. The educated are in most cases killing the uneducated! Put that in your pipe and smoke it. Perhaps all this is what your 'Daily Hack' should be investigating and exposing, rather than the latest spat between footballers' wives or the members of the royal family?

Roger sighs, he's tired of all this thinking. But I'm not finished.

To resume our argument at the beginning, Roger: In the one-hundred strong, knife-wielding, torch-carrying, bloodthirsty mob heading to your home to burn it down with you and your family within, do you think there is one man, two, ten who remembers our equation and will try and introduce a degree of reason and justice into the proceedings? In the western movies you love so much, perhaps, a truth-loving, reasonable man with a strong sense of justice will appear and dissuade them. In real life, this does not happen …

So, the difference between me and the members of your mob, starts Roger …

… is that at least you have me to stop you, if not the others, for it is too late for them.

So then, my spectator, my conscience, my inner voice, my royal pain in the arse, where do we stand, you and I, asks Roger? Are we adversaries or allies? I still struggle to understand our bond.

I think we might portray our mutual existence as a dialogue if we are to convince anyone that our relationship is also the source of reason and justice, in any case. For reason, which tends to the truth (whether accepted is another question; it is usually the beginning of a new round of reason and another truth which shall probably have to undergo yet again the test of reason, depending on the complexity of the question in hand) can only manifest itself in the opposition of arguments, or facts, of course. We know that 2+2 equals 4 (excuse me for going back to my mantra again!), because we can see that 2+2 doesn't equal 5, nor 3, for that matter.

And justice, asks Roger?

Ah, justice! You do well to ask, my boy. If most if not all the conflicts and wars and mass murders and genocide going on in our little world are based on lies, are justified and defended by outrageous trickery and deception (examine their origins closely and you will inevitably come to this conclusion), where does justice find its place? I'll tell you … Justice is our solemn, eternal promise to the innocent to identify those who have aggrieved and injured them and to bring them to account. Truth and reason are its handmaidens.

Well, that's straightforward, then, Roger tells me sarcastically. The world's problems resolved.

No, I tell him, the world's problems identified, not resolved. Because though man has a peculiar passion to punish the others—and punishment is not justice but that which, in the best of cases, follows its due process—his ardour and devotion to justice is not evident at all. As long as his own person, his own case, is not involved, of course. Otherwise, he does not lose a lot of sleep about the question. And despite all the desperate hope that bringing criminals to justice will dissuade others from walking the same path to infamy, it never has and never will. It is actually a huge paradox which would make one laugh if so much suffering were not involved: To believe that knowledge of the fate that will face you will hold anyone back from committing a crime is to equip with reason a man on the precipice of a precisely unreasoned act! We must of course keep up this pretence, if only to avoid a sense of complete helplessness in the face of evil. All the while embracing with our hearts and souls the real meaning of justice: to render our profound respect and remembrance to crime's victims.

Give me a break, would you, now, Roger pleads? My head is spinning and I really can't go on with this discussion right now. Too many abstract notions at once for a modest boy like me.

Right, I agree for today. Concentrate rather on your amorous affairs for the while. Think hard of something perceptive and intelligent to say to the lady to excuse your wretchedness. I hope that I have given you a few ideas on which to build.

Yes, I remember that day very fondly. In a way, it was the beginning of a new man's life. It's only a pity that I couldn't restrain myself from ending our discussion with the question that I am determined he should answer.

And so, Roger, have you destroyed anyone's life?

The virtues of bashing immigrants

The big chief has summoned Roger again this morning.

"What's your team working on, then?" Bowdler asks as Roger pokes his head through the door. "Sit down."

"We've got a couple of things on the go."

"I bloody well hope so, but what are they? You've been racking up a hell of a bill these last couple of weeks. Ruinous. They'd better be something good."

"Well, it's all a bit speculative for the moment," says Roger.

"We need something big, you know," says the Chief Editor mildly. "Something a bit different. Our readers are showing signs they've had enough of politics for a while. Single copy sales, not to mention web traffic, have been dropping off badly on some days of the week. I'm beginning to think they don't give a toss any longer who's running the country."

"I can sympathize," says Roger unadvisedly.

"I don't want your bloody sympathy, nor do our readers," Bowdler retorts. I think he's trying to work himself up into anger. It's clear he feels a lot better—perhaps it's physiological?—when he's in a rage and can start shouting.

"I just mean that we're becoming difficult to follow. We've changed our mind three times now about who we're backing for the leadership."

"And don't I bloody well know it!" says Bowdler. "His Highness changes horse every week, depending on where he spent the previous weekend and who was there to get his ear."

"How is our dear proprietor, these days?"

Bowdler ignores Roger's impertinent question.

"So, what is it you're working on? I need something *really* scandalous to get the attention of our readers again."

"Well, one investigation is about how we're apparently

letting immigrants into the country without even bothering to check their backgrounds, as the rules require."

Bowdler visibly cheers up and leans forward. They haven't bashed any immigrants for several weeks now, it's true. But he wants to know: "Who made those rules? Who can we blame that they're impractical, useless, that they didn't bother to put the mechanisms in place to actually apply them? Or that they did, and there's a conspiracy in the civil service, perhaps even the police, to ignore them?"

"It was a good while ago, a previous government," Roger assures him. "Not our lot; they just inherited the rules and the immigrants who bypassed them, out of incompetence, or perhaps corruption? We're looking into all the options."

"Good," says Bowdler. "And we need, of course, a few unchecked psychopaths and rapists, a killer or two would be great, as examples of maniacs we let in to commit more crimes and defile our soil. Whether they raped and murdered before they got here or after. The ideal would be both, that goes without saying."

"We're onto it."

"And the other story?"

"Links between the Assad regime in Syria—they're the bad guys, the last time we checked foreign affairs—and one of our companies specialising in biotech. It all came from your vapour trail idea, boss. That was a good hunch."

Flattery, flattery, I whisper disapprovingly to Roger.

"Yes, I suspected there was something there. But what's biotech?"

"It covers a variety of sins, mostly innocuous, but clearly also the nasty stuff, making biological weapons, for instance, spreading death and disease."

"Well, go ahead on that too, but be quick about it. And don't forget that it's the local angle that counts. No one very much gives a shit that Assad is killing his own people or gassing rebels, least of all *our* readers, of course, but if we're indeed in on the game, that might have the makings of something we can really blow up. Where did we stand with those bastards when all this may have happened, though?"

"We have, let's say, a very fluctuating relationship with the Syrian regime," says Roger. "A few years back, the late Queen even invited Assad for tea, with the Missus."

"Well, you can leave *that* out," says Bowdler, with a black look that Roger well understands means he will brook no discussion on this matter.

As we leave the Chief Editor's office, Roger mutters to me, What an arsehole.

Yes, my boy, indeed! I'm glad that you feel that way. You're coming on, you know. The arsehole in question used to be your hero …

A stockbroker or a pimp

So, dear reader, are you of a romantic disposition? Are you impatient to hear how Roger P., ace reporter of the scabrous 'Daily Hack', destroyer of reputations and perhaps lives, won the heart and hand of lettered, clever, cultivated Sandra P., a humane, compassionate young woman radically engaged in the fight against the disgraceful conduct of the country's affairs, the unshakeable grip on the national psyche of the tabloid media, and the unstoppable plunge into intellectual and cultural mediocrity of our long-suffering people?

In a way, the most difficult and at the same time most superficial obstacle to their immortal, undying love (let's face it, one repeatedly embarks on such stories with the profound belief that they will be eternal, however comical such convictions usually turn out to prove in retrospect) has already been hurdled with ease: To put it rather crudely, if I may, they fancy each other. A look, a touch or two, a complicit smile, had settled that question beyond discussion somewhere in the dark alleys between the 'Ws' and the 'Bs'.

You think that my observations on the sacred matter of love are flippant, perhaps? If this is so, it is nature, not I, that has nevertheless decided that what I am telling you is true. You can love everything about a man or a woman, but without this *animal* (as I once described it) instinct that brings you together, you are destined rather to be friends. If, of course, such uncarnal relationships are your cup of tea.

But attraction is fragile and a woman is often reluctant, particularly she who knows a thing or two about the male. At least a woman like Sandra P., in my estimation and in Roger's too. Until now, he has found it far too easy to seduce, bed and leave his conquests. Most have not cared that he did so, in truth, but there have surely been a few broken hearts or, if hearts don't break in our times, some seriously injured pride along the way.

In any case, Roger is now heading for the bookshop again. It is just two days since he bought and then consumed his Böll and his Waugh. He has yet no precise idea what he is doing, like an inebriated and slightly desperate man stumbling ever deeper into the night in the vague hope that something meaningful still might happen to him before dawn.

He turns, of course, to me for advice.

Shouldn't you have figured all this out before you set off, Roger, I ask him? You'll likely not get two opportunities to comprehensively foul this up. I know you. You'll feel completely humiliated if she greets you coldly and sends you packing. You're not used to defeat, to being refused, to not getting your way. Your charm may have worked a treat with all your models and actresses but perhaps they were after something from you and the 'Hack' in return for their attentions? Perhaps you have until now only had to deal with ladies as much on the make as you yourself?

Yes, he replies, ignoring my slurs about the authenticity of his charm, perhaps I should have stayed at home until I had a strategy. But I still can't see what I could have come up with.

So, you'll just blunder into the shop and ask for some new book recommendations? A romance or two, to indicate your mood?

Get lost, says Roger. Are you with me or against me? You continue to be very ambiguous about that, my dear *conscience,* my *inner voice,* my *spectator,* or whatever the hell you want to call yourself.

Yes, I quite like the man, I've always suspected that I might, given time. I like that he has some fight in him, wants to engage me, is growing stronger in standing up to me. Let's see what happens. After all, Miss Sandra is not the last good woman he will ever set his eyes on and, indeed, rejection might even do him some good.

Roger can't resist a stop by the Red Lion for a shot or three.

"What are *you* all tarted up for then, darlin'?" asks his favourite tavernkeeper. "New haircut, sharp suit, pink shirt —you look like a stockbroker. Or a pimp."

Roger says nothing, just indicates twice that he wants his glass refilled and slugs each of the drinks down like one of his favourite saloon gunslingers.

"Mind your own business and don't forget to change the sign," says Roger, walking straight out of the establishment again after throwing a banknote down on the counter. "The *Philistine,* you remember?" He doesn't wait for a reply and is already off down the street, hurrying towards his fate.

Roger catches sight of Sandra through the shopfront window. She smiles. You see, she hasn't forgotten me at all, he tells me.

You have commanded me to keep silent, I remind him. You're on your own now.

"Well, well. You've finished those books already, then?" Sandra asks him as he enters the shop.

"Yes, indeed. They were great recommendations, thanks so much! I came to ask if you had any events, book readings, for example, that I might join and learn something?"

Humility. From my Roger. That's quite new. And what an inspiration to ask about readings.

"Nothing coming up any time soon," says Sandra. "Do you like listening to authors presenting and discussing their writing, then?"

"I don't know, to tell the truth. All this is quite new to me. I lead a very empty life in many ways and really haven't taken time to read much, not since I left school, actually, which wasn't yesterday, as you can see. I've been quite sheltered from the world of culture, of literature, and would like to do something about it. I want to learn."

A frowning Sandra looks at him in slight bewilderment, as though Kasper Hauser had just walked in the door. She's clearly not used to such confessions from grown men and perhaps doesn't know what to say. Later she would admit that his meekness and honesty had quite thrown her; it was completely out of key with his appearance. He looked so *slick*, she would say, yes, that was the word.

"Dear me," says Sandra, after a moment or two, brightening up and smiling again. "You *are* a suitable case for treatment, aren't you? Where can we possibly start?"

Roger likes that 'we', as though she has already embraced his problem for herself.

"I could, needless to say, give you all manner of suggestions about what you might read, but I personally don't believe at all in recommending books to other people. Unless you know them really intimately, it's quite useless."

Though I had promised to keep silent, I intervene very sharply anyhow, because I know what Roger P. is going to say next and I have to stop him. No, Roger! No, no, no. Hold your tongue and do not under any circumstances say "We could certainly arrange *that*." He keeps quiet.

The lady continues. "Yes, I'm convinced that books must be meaningful in some way for you personally, perhaps answer some of the questions you've been asking yourself, if your ambition is to enrich your understanding of people, of the world, in any case."

"Oh yes, that's exactly my ambition, you couldn't have expressed it more clearly. I want to learn more about ... about ... *the human condition*, yes, that's how I could put it very broadly."

"Splendid, splendid," says Sandra approvingly. "We cannot help to improve the world if we don't even try and understand man and what drives him, can we?"

"Indeed, indeed," says Roger. "But perhaps something with a little hope in it? Something optimistic?" (That surprises me; where did he get that, I ask myself?)

At that moment in the conversation, another man walks in the shop and clearly wants to talk to Sandra.

"I'll be with you in just a moment," she tells the man, who nods and wanders off down an alley. And then quietly to Roger: "There's a fellow you'd want to know. He's a writer! A real living author of novels that sell in my shop! Brilliant, quite brilliant; he knows great literature much better even than I do. He's very charming and humble with it, too."

Come off it, Roger, you are not going to feel pangs of jealousy, are you, I mock him? The pangs have indeed been activated and Roger feels a little sick in the chest. Here is a man with whom he cannot possibly compete in any way; he's not used to that.

But at that moment, something quite unexpected happens.

"Why don't you take me for a drink some time and we can discuss all this?" says Sandra.

Ah, the blessings of equality between men and women in our time! *She* was asking *him* out.

Well, not 'out', really, Roger; a literary encounter, let's say. All your problems remain, of course; you still have to explain your miserable life, but you're way ahead of where you were when we came in. Good for you, I tell him.

Sandra had clearly been anxious to go and take care of her author and had suggested that Roger should write his name and telephone number down at the cash desk; she would call him.

And then she hastened off.

The plot thickens

Charlie comes in this morning to report on his Assad work.

"This better be good," says Roger. "It seems the readers are getting bored with our current fare and need some new doses of shock and horror to occupy their sorry lives."

Steady on, Roger, I tell him. At 'The Daily Hack', we admire and respect our readers. Don't belittle them in front of underlings, or you'll be heading for trouble. Only Bowdler is allowed to insult them, because he insults the whole human race, indistinctly. Charlie knows the rules; we don't want him suggesting to anyone that you're going through a moral crisis, do we? Haha!

Roger suggests that I allow him to get on with his business without further 'heckling', as he puts it. I'll do my best.

"Well, you know what it's like, boss, one never knows how these things will turn out or whether they mean anything—particularly when you still haven't really told me yet what story we are actually working on with this."

Roger ignores his fishing and motions for him to go on.

"Here's what I've got, in any case. I tracked down Baker's children, a son and a daughter. They both live near the former family farm where he knocked himself off. The bloke told me that he wouldn't talk to anyone from 'that shitful rag'—he was referring to our esteemed newspaper—and that I could get stuffed. His daughter, though, invited me in for a cup of tea and poured her heart out. It cost me four cups of the revolting stuff; I hate tea."

"Get on with it, then. I don't need this in episodes. Just tell me what she told you."

"Right. Daphne—that's her name—said that neither she nor her brother believed the suicide story. The usual stuff. He wasn't the kind of man to kill himself. He loved his children—he was a widower—more than anything in the world and would at the very least have left them a note if he had done it. He wasn't depressed at all; had been his usual cheerful self when they had seen him the previous day; and bla-bla-bla. Like so many suicides, no one saw it coming, most especially those close to the deceased. In short, there was no material evidence that it was anything else but suicide, just the intimate conviction of his children. That didn't stop them making a big fuss with the police, though, and then at the inquest, which is how their suspicions ended up briefly in the media. They demanded that the police investigate what their father was working on, for example. They knew his job was very 'hush-hush', as Daphne put it, that he travelled a lot, and that much of what he did was 'top secret'. The police told her that since there were no reasons at all to suspect that the death was unusual—they suggested it might be put down to his grief over the death of her mother the previous year, despite the fact that he'd never shown any—they were not going to meddle in such matters. And that was that. They had no one to turn to with their questions after that, and so just dropped the whole thing."

"That's all?"

"No. Because by the third cup of the delightful lady's disgusting tea, she told me that a few days after the funeral she got a call and then a visit from one of her father's colleagues

—none other than Archie Samuels. He asked to meet at the farm, Baker's home, that is, and shortly after he got there started to poke around."

"Poke around?"

"Yup. He told Daphne that her father used to take some of his files out of the office to work on at weekends. If there were any at the farm, the Institute would like them back, for the records, if nothing else, he said. She didn't see any harm in it, so he filled a few boxes from the stacks in Baker's study, put them in his car and drove off with them. She said that the stuff included a lot of professional photographs that Archie said would be useful when they came to write the history of her father's Institute. Then, boss, I asked whether any of them were those on her late father's Facebook page, which had never been taken down. She laughed her head off about that one, our Daphne. Her father's Facebook page? Hahaha. He probably hadn't even heard of Facebook, let alone having a so-called page. So I showed her. 'Herbert E. Baker, A Life in Pictures' it's called. Photo after photo, with no captions and no comments, posted by someone with a pseudonym; at least there's no proper name. She recognized a few of them as coming from those strewn around her father's bureau. She had never examined any of them closely. Not seen Assad, I guess, though I thought it best not to mention that one. Perhaps she recognized him, perhaps she didn't. In any case, she was really stunned that someone had set this up, presumably *after* her father's death. It seems she doesn't frequent Facebook either."

"So, if we put 2 and 2 together," says Roger, "it's Archie who's running this Facebook page in remembrance of his predecessor."

"I'd say so," Charlie says. "We have no way of checking, though. And it seems pretty weird that he would reveal that his own previous boss, his own employer, was gallivanting with that son of a bitch in Syria. Wouldn't it?"

"Indeed," is all Roger says. "Indeed." And then, after a pause, "What pseudonym is the poster using, by the way?"

"Utagho. U-t-a-g-h-o. Meaningless as far as I know. Where do we go with this now, boss?"

"I've no idea, Charlie. Good work in any case. Take a couple of days off and I'll get back to you."

Charlie smiles, thanks Roger, and scampers out the door before he has a chance to change his mind.

A most dreadful confession

I suspect the guards here think that Roger is crazy. They are very kind about it, though, on the whole. All diligent readers of 'The Daily Hack', they seem rather fascinated that they have one of its star reporters under their personal locks and keys, however bonkers he may be.

"Writing your memoirs, then?" one of them asks this morning, seeing him talking to himself and scribbling as usual.

"Something like that," smiles Roger. "I'll send you a signed copy when they're published."

"You're including all the gory details of your killings, I hope," the man says cheerfully.

"You can count on it," Roger replies.

You will, won't you? he asks me.

Naturally. That will be the fun part, I tell him.

For now, though, I must write about the day Roger faced up to himself, finally held himself to account, took stock of his life, examined properly the charges of superficiality, ignorance, immorality, mendaciousness, frippery, insincerity, *lack of humanity* that I have been levelling at him for so long.

In truth, of course, you don't just sit down one fine day and go through the ledgers and balance sheets of your life like an auditor might do with the company books. Only in literature does one encounter such experiences. If it were that straightforward, after all, we would likely see mass, overnight conversions to rectitude and honesty and new lives blossoming all over the place like flowers in the spring.

So if, dear reader, as an upstanding citizen, you are looking forward to hearing about the dark night of the soul from which a radiant Roger, incandescent in the fine habits of his new self, finally emerged to the blinding light of day, I shall have to disappoint you. One epiphany is pretty much all you get in a life, and Roger had used up his at an uncommonly early age.

While on the subject of 2+2, though, I think we can comfortably employ this truth of all truths, the truth from which all others follow, in describing the method with which Roger went about his self-inquisition that day.

He was not starting from afresh, of course. For several years, as I have told you, I have been insinuating doubt at every opportunity into the multiple recesses and tunnels that not only Roger but every man has burrowed deep down in the immense penumbra of his mind. This is where our traumas go and hide, perhaps, and where they should stay, if we are able to ignore the foolish advice of a certain school of psychoanalysis that proposes we should drag them out and start suffering from them all over again. Be that as it may, it is in these dark, hidden corners that our doubts have a tendency to conceal themselves too and where, if we dare, we must dispatch our questions to ferret them out and get to grips with them.

Over time, Roger had stuffed and crammed his countless existential misgivings into every vacant nook and cranny of his skull. It goes without saying that none were beyond my reach, though, and I relentlessly sought them out to tease and trouble him anew. My ambition was not, of course, to transform him in one fell swoop into a decent human. Men are not like that and the light of goodness in the best of cases will only dawn on them very gradually. That was all I was aiming for, really. To keep the questions alive long enough in the tunnels of his mind that little by little he must deal with them and in doing so enlighten himself and eventually change. He knew that, in the meantime, they were going nowhere, because I was preventing that from happening.

What was special about that day of all days that he should undertake his *aggiornamento* over breakfast? He had barely slept and was mentally fragile, which is always a good condition in which to be for such a discussion with yourself, since your bad faith is exhausted too and will put up little resistance. At least this is what he discovered.

You guessed, of course, that it was the day of his first date with Sandra. She had left it a full week before calling him and even then said she wasn't available for another seven or eight days. As consolation he had talked her into having lunch with him rather than the 'drink' she proposed.

Old Roger behaved very comically as he waited for the great day to come round. She had asked to meet somewhere near her bookshop, since she couldn't be away more than a couple of hours at most (even this sounded to him like a gift from heaven), so he set about finding the right restaurant in her part of town. He had lunch at no less than three of them to see if they were good enough for the woman of his life. In each of them, he changed table twice in search of the quietest corner. He over-ate in all, appraising several dishes, and put the waiting staff to test by changing his mind about some of them, to observe their reaction. It was the second of the three that won his verdict and he booked his chosen table for the day, telling the head man discreetly that he was not to recognize him because he had never been there before, slipping a handsome bank note into his hand as he did so. The man took it as much in his stride as if he had been asked the time of day. Obviously, such shenanigans were common.

Today is finally the day. Roger arrives half an hour before the appointed time. The head man greets him kindly, but with no familiarity nor even a wink or a complicitous nod. He deserves another note if he keeps this up to the end, thinks Roger. And right on time, after he has had two large whiskies and told the waiter to take the glass away, the lady walks in. They have omitted to exchange family names, but happily Sandra spots him in the corner, points and walks straight over. They shake hands softly; a tingle runs up Roger's spine.

Roger reminds me a little aggressively that I have agreed to take a walk, as far as that is possible.

You are on your own, I tell him. I don't know how you're going to get through this, but good luck!

They exchange full names and niceties. Sandra congratulates him for the wonderful choice of restaurant. She has heard great good spoken of it, but has never been there before. Roger says that he just happened to chance upon it one time he was in the neighbourhood and made a note to lunch there one day. He hopes it will be satisfactory.

When they have settled down, ordered their dishes, and have sat smiling at each other for a few moments, Sandra, not unnaturally, asks Roger to tell her something about himself. Apart from being a novice in literary matters, she smiles, what does he do for a living? Roger takes the plunge.

"I have a confession to make. You may be shocked."

Now how do you suppose, dear reader, the lady reacts? Does she tell him she's not a priest, perhaps? Or say she hopes that it's not *too shocking*—that he's on the run from the police, that he has three wives, or a dreadful contagious disease.

None of this. The lady just smiles gently. Not a word. Roger swoons, though perhaps it was the whisky on an empty stomach; the sensation is the same as that of early love, after all.

"Have you a little time to hear me out?" asks Roger. "You're not going to be very happy with what I tell you."

Again, Sandra just smiles wordlessly.

"Do you remember those books you sold me? Well, they've been a wake-up call for me."

"That's wonderful. I don't often hear *that*. The power of great literature really is underestimated, you know. Personally, I loved the Böll when I read it many moons ago. Devastating for the tabloid press, don't you think? Yet here we are fifty years later completely in its grip still. Can you possibly explain it?"

"Perhaps no one read the book here," Roger ventures. "No one who didn't already hate these newspapers, like you, for instance."

"True enough," says Sandra. "I don't imagine that many of the readers of our trash tabloids are very much into modern German literature. More's the pity."

Roger gets a brief respite as the dishes begin to arrive and wine is served.

Get it over with, get it done, I urge him, despite my promises to keep quiet.

"I work for 'The Daily Hack'," says Roger suddenly. "This is my confession. I don't know how I ended up there. I know that sounds rather stupid, but I was practically a child when I started and one thing just followed another. I'm now Investigations Editor. I'm not proud of it. I haven't done anything against my will. So I'm fully responsible. You're right when you say it's all trash, I see that now, though it's taken time. I thought that if the people wanted it, then it could only be good. No one forces them to buy us. Can the people be wrong? Good, respectable, decent folk living all over the country."

Sandra's smile hasn't deserted her, remarkably. Roger has had visions of soup thrown in his face, smashed glasses, chairs tossed aside, insults, accusations. He had been ready to deal with all that. But here she was silently smiling at him. It was hard to handle.

"I understand if you wish to leave right away," he offers.

"When did you begin to doubt that what you're doing is a decent way to spend your life?" she asks, ignoring his remark. "When did you see that the 'Hack', like the others but a bit worse, is simply trash, to use your own word, and no good to anyone, least of all to the people who buy it?"

Why the hell is she remaining so calm and equanimous and kind, he asks me?

Perhaps that's her nature, I suggest?

"It's taken time, too much time," he begins. "They took me on when I was barely out of school, for some of the dirty jobs that I don't care for the moment to talk about, and then fairly quickly for the bigger stories. If you set aside morals and ethics and truth-seeking, as I see now that we do, it's not hard to progress rapidly within the paper, because the level of talent is very low; I'm surrounded by mediocrities, really. I am a mediocrity myself, of course, I agree with you there, if that's what you're thinking. Anyhow, I got caught up in it all. My byline all over the place—instant fame. The hunt for the scoop. The generous expenses to take actresses and secretaries to restaurants to grill them about their boyfriends and bosses. Recognition and secretive phone calls from members of the government hoping to get a leg up in their careers by denouncing their colleagues' improprieties and peccadillos; and so on and so on. I thought, and this was perhaps my biggest mistake, that I was actually closer to *what was going on*, closer to the *truth*—believe it or not—than anybody else. I and my colleagues actually look down on everybody, can you believe that? We have this sense that we somehow run society, run the nation. The power that we have has completely gone to our heads. We actually believe all this!"

"And you don't any longer. But you're still there," says Sandra quietly.

"It's a drug. It's hardly a revelation, I know, but power is a drug. When we think of power, few think of journalists, but we have more than anyone else at all, because we control or heavily influence people's knowledge and perceptions of what they take for reality. We are *there* to tell them what happened—and *they aren't*—and into the bargain we even tell them what to think about it. There was once a time, I suppose, when most of the things a man or woman knew and talked about came from personal experience, from his or her own life. That was the time before mass media, of course. Now, practically everything people think they know comes from someone else, is second or third hand; and they mainly get it from people like me who pump information and opinion day and night into their skulls."

"Haven't the internet and social media largely changed that?" asks Sandra. "Now we have thousands of information sources and opinions about everything. Your monopoly has crumbled, hasn't it? And your power along with it? Hasn't that created a brave new world in itself?"

"Perhaps you are right," Roger concedes. "Perhaps we journalists haven't sufficiently noticed it, yet. We can still make and break mere politicians, those who think they have the power monopoly, though. We can even destroy the rich, the famous in most any walk of life, if the desire comes over us. The internet and social media have rather aided and abetted us in that more than anything else."

"Does that desire come over *you* very much?"

"He's asked me often whether I've ever destroyed anyone's life."

"He?"

Christ, Roger, don't bring me into this!

"Did I say 'he'?" Roger laughs. "Don't worry, I don't usually talk about myself in the third person. Slip of the tongue."

"That's quite a question, though," says Sandra gravely. "Have you?"

"Not that I know. Though to be honest I've not yet

thought about it an awful lot. Of course, we don't always get to hear about what happens to the subjects—*victims*, if you like—of our stories, if they're not celebrities or famous in one way or another. If they're just ordinary people, for example ... But I'm really trying to make a good faith effort to examine the consequences of my work and I can't in all truth say that I've personally created too much suffering. Who knows? What I'm beginning to see, though, is that we and our colleagues create a very unhelpful and unhealthy *climate* in the country. Against immigrants, against people on benefits, against other nations, against anything even vaguely resembling reasonable, calm debate, against those—experts, for example—who do actually know what they're talking about, against thinkers and intellectuals of all stripes, against the institutions of state, against serious culture ... We encourage contempt and hysteria and anger at everyone, or at least that's how it seems when I'm able to distance myself from it all and look at matters with a certain neutrality."

Sandra, the darling, is listening intently and, apparently, approving what she is hearing. After a few minutes, as they by tacit agreement also eat, in silence, she speaks again.

"One of the many things that it's particularly difficult to stomach about your newspaper is its slavish, obsequious, profoundly indecent support for this and previous governments. It's not so much that you are disgustingly right-wing, but that you deliberately twist and deform and lie yourselves into unconditional and blind cheerleading for absolutely anything they do. I'm an adult and I know that people have different political sensibilities and ideas and that's just perfectly normal and it's fine that many of them are contrary to my own beliefs. But you at the 'Hack' aren't at all in the business of simply laying out the arguments for your ideology and letting people consider them. You are trying to defame and dirty anyone at all who has different opinions while being accomplices in the deceit and travesties of your favourites. I'm told that this country's press was once admired abroad, not least by writers and journalists, for its separation of fact and opinion and its fair play. What a joke that is today! This is not the only matter in which we have pulled the wool over the eyes of the world we still—unbelievably—think we are *leading,* though God knows where. Look at our politicians! Do you imagine that such a comprehensive collection of mediocrities and liars could be in power in any other half-developed democracy? And do you know what, Roger? I do believe that it's you and your rabid rag that have brought things to such an incredibly low level and are keeping them there."

Well, dear reader, I did tell you that the lady was *engaged,* didn't I?

The most amazing thing about Sandra's little speech, for Roger, was that it was not spoken in anger. How on earth can one be so passionate without raising one's voice or otherwise manifesting signs of rage? No, she had set out her thoughts with complete equanimity and even ended them with a delicious ironic smile. He was in love. Again, still, even more than before! To the extent that he got completely carried away and said:

"If you sit there smiling at me much longer and saying nothing, I'll have to ask you to marry me, you know."

With this poignant outburst, I shall leave our love interlude for the while—after all, romance bores a lot of people, you must admit it—and get on with our story.

We do not publish in Pottsville

Bowdler has called a general editorial meeting today. There's a lot of speculation in the newsroom about why he wants to talk to us, particularly since he's excluded all technical, art and graphic staff from attending, which is unusual.

Pep talks aren't Bowdler's thing, so the consensus is that we're in for a *bollocking* of one kind or another. Falling circulation and web traffic, perhaps, or the lack of scoops and exclusives and *juicy scandals,* as he likes to call them. Or perhaps he wants to share his latest conspiracy with us and set the whole place onto its investigation.

All of us are certain of only one thing: Bowdler is in a foul, black mood and clearly looking to wind himself up into a fully-fledged rage at our expense.

"I've spent the last couple of days doing nothing but read your crummy stories," he begins. "No wonder our sales are dropping off. Nothing for anyone to get their teeth into at all. But it's not that I want to talk about; you know all that as well as I do. Here's what's causing our readers to flee—your fucking vocabulary!"

Everybody looks at someone else; a few giggles are barely suppressed.

"Here, I'll show you something." And at that, he stretches his arm to a table next to him and grabs a colleague's coffee mug.

"What did I just do, Barton?" he asks.

"Stole my coffee," says Barton.

"And how did I do that?"

"You just reached out and grabbed it."

"Exactly. I couldn't have said it better. Now, here I have a story that you Barton wrote yesterday, the one about the singer accused of racist lyrics, in which you write that you '*reached out*' to her agent for a comment. I assume he was standing next to you?"

Bowdler looks slowly around the room, glaring at one reporter after the other, before turning back to Barton and shouting in his face: "You did not fucking *reach out* to her agent. You contacted or called him or sent him a carrier pigeon, I don't know. But under no circumstances did you fucking *reach out* to anyone. I will not have that shit language in my newspaper, do you hear me? I am sick and tired of all this fucking Americanese all over 'The Daily Hack'. We write in English, here."

He paused for breath, now red in the face, before going on.

"So, Julie, the former Chairman of the Liberals *passed away* on Tuesday? No he fucking did not! He did not pass away, pass, pass on, pass sideways, pass out or pass up or do any passing at all, he just fucking *died*; as long as I'm Chief Editor, people *die*!"

No one ever replies, unless asked, when Bowdler goes on such a rampage, so the guilty only look at their shoes.

"We do not have *go-to* solutions, ideas, food, or anything else. Only the Americans say such stupid, crass things, not us. When someone is killed, I do not want to hear about how the police talked to his *loved ones*. What the fuck do you know about *that*? Half of them probably hated his guts. Respect the language, for Christ's sake. While I'm on the subject, could someone explain why you have all banished the lovely word *mother* from your stories? If I see another one of you writing about this or that '*mum*' I'll have you shot! And you, Fenton," he addresses our top sports writer, "I have here a piece you wrote on rugby in which you say, I quote: '*Going forward*, the players will all wear their names on their shirts'. Tell me, Fenton, what will they wear when they're going backwards, or sideways?"

Fenton mumbles that he used the term to mean 'in future'. It was common nowadays.

"When you mean 'in future', you will fucking write 'in future'!" Bowdler shouts. "We do not publish for the people of fucking Pottsville!"

Bowdler's rant seems to have run its course as he turns away from the room and starts fiddling with his papers. We all get up quietly and begin to move to the door when he gets his second breath and yells after us: "And if you want some *quality time,* as you Helen, wrote in your dumb column yesterday, or are *seeking closure,* as you Keith wrote that some crime victim's family or other were doing, you can go and work on the fucking 'New York Times!' I do not ever want to see such expressions again in my paper."

Roger, and perhaps some of the others, is staggered by this speech. Who would have guessed that old Bowdler would harbour such hatred and resentment in a matter of language?

I admire him for all that, Roger tells me. You really never know everything about a man, do you? He's a scab on the face of humanity, that goes without saying, but that he should care about preserving the English language like that really must go down to his credit.

'*Cada loco con su tema*', my boy. Every madman has his subject, as the Spanish say. Let's not grace him with the mantle of insanity, though. He's only a very ordinary shit with a certain respect for words, if none at all for people. A man is a prisoner of his vocabulary, Roger, did you notice that? Not only in the range of things he is able to express, but in the way it sets not only the tenor but the limits of his thoughts. It's precisely for this reason that I've always pushed you to break out of your established circle of words that can only turn and turn around the same ideas. And if you don't have the words and ideas to occupy your mind, you can eat yourself alive with untold anguish. It's amazing, don't you think, how the enemies of clear thought in our own country have stigmatized those who express themselves with versatility and depth?

Back to the books, then, laughs Roger.

Smashing children against trees

Marjorie has called Roger and asked for a meeting. She's heard back from Cambodia and says that they're maybe on to something.

"So, did we find his trace?" asks Roger, inviting her to sit down.

"Our 'Sok Charya' probably doesn't exist. It's a very common name and our man, the one we've hired, that is, didn't even bother to try and track any of them down. He did much better, though. He figured that few Cambodians could get rich in business, as we told him he had, and remain out of public view. At the same time, something struck him about the timing of this Sok's exile. His departure coincides pretty much with the creation of the war crimes tribunal in Cambodia. Quite a few prominent people appear to have 'disappeared' around about then ..."

"It took *thirty years* after the genocide to set up a tribunal?" asks Roger.

"Yes, indeed. And even then, they only found five people to judge, three of whom died before they got round to it. They don't seem very assiduous to bring their butchers in for the reckoning, to say the least."

"And our Sok?"

"Our man in Phnom Penh, who is well connected with the foreign Embassies and thus has a way to get to the tribunal investigators—it's all a mixed UN-Cambodia process—has procured a long list of the people who were wanted when they began their work all that time ago. Happily, it includes photos of most of them. He's sent it over ... and we've taken a picture of your neighbour."

"How did you do *that*?"

"Bill was in the neighbourhood and hid in the woods behind your homes," Marjorie smiled.

"You could have asked me first, you know."

"You were otherwise engaged and we didn't have time. Bill was due on another job. Anyhow, he didn't have to wait long. Mister so-called Sok was gardening and he shot away."

"And?"

"To cut a long story short, we ran a facial through the recognition software—or something like that, the photo boys have the details—and your chap resembles one of the wanted. A certain Khieu Sen. We're far from certain, because there's a difference of twenty years between the photos, at least, and the technology can be a bit dodgy. It's not like DNA analysis."

"And what's this Khieu accused of exactly?"

"He was apparently a key figure in one of the death camps, the 'killing fields', as you will remember they were called. A senior officer in the special branch, which was in charge of internal security. He's on the wanted list for so many crimes, that I can't even remember them all. Genocide, crimes against humanity, war crimes, rape, murder, torture. He liked to get personally engaged, as it were. One of his specialities was smashing babies and children against trees to break their heads open."

"Jesus," is all Roger can think to say. "Jesus wept."

They both stare at their shoes for a minute or two.

"Why wasn't this beast picked up before?" asks Roger finally.

"I have no idea. Everything got very murky and complicated when the Khmer Rouge were kicked out and the Vietnamese took over. Do you know which side we took? Got it in one: we backed the genocide perpetrators. Our Prime Minister at the time even said she thought there were 'reasonable elements' in the Khmer Rouge who 'we could work with'. And together with the US we backed these murderous bastards for at least twenty years afterwards as they waged war with the Viets. And even supported them in keeping their seat at the United Nations. So it's not all that surprising that thousands of war criminals got lost in the woods, as it were."

"Indeed," says Roger. "Marx and the others were wrong with their clever aphorisms. History repeats itself, full stop. It was the same after the Second World War. In Germany, in Japan too. Punishing the killers was the least of our concerns. A few show trials and that was that. The Cambodians, with our assistance, have just gone one worse, that's all. No one tried at all for thirty years afterwards to bring any murderers to account, apparently."

This is the Roger P. I like. Thoughtful. Caring. He's really coming on, this boy. We'll make a humanist of him yet.

"What do we know about this Khieu Sen since those days?" Roger asks Marjorie.

"That'll cost us another five thousand to find out. If there's anything to find, that is. That's our man's price."

"I'll have to pass that one through Bowdler. We've reached our budget limit for the moment. I'll get back to you."

"In the meantime, boss, do you mind if I look further into the photo business? I thought I'd contact some of those Cambodian groups here to see if they recognize him."

"OK. Just be very, very careful please, Marjorie. I'm sure that the nebulous web of exile groups includes opponents and supporters, as they always do. Make it very discreet and make absolutely certain you get the right guys. If this Khieu is by any chance our Sok—and I know that remains a very long shot—I don't even know whether that makes him for or against the current regime or for or against the various oppositions. Advance very prudently. We don't want to alert anyone, least of all Sok, to what we're up to, so never mention his current name to anyone, just in case. One last thing, Marjorie—stop calling me 'boss' will you?"

Marjorie smiles and suddenly remembers to tell Roger, "One thing I forgot to tell you. When Bill was setting up his stuff in the woods, a friendly Labrador jumped out of nowhere and dropped a bone in his lap. Bill didn't want to draw any attention to himself, so stuffed it in his camera bag. He told me to ask if you wanted perhaps to take it back?"

Roger laughs. "It's not such a bad idea, actually, since it often distracts the dog from chewing me. But tell Bill I'll pass anyhow, thanks."

Who cares about genocide?

Perhaps, dear reader, you are tired of our narratory circumvolutions and would like to move on straight away to learn how Bowdler reacted when told of the burgeoning Cambodian budget? I suspected as much.

I remember the day well; it was one of Roger's finest, when all is said and done. He managed even to surprise me, which is a rare enough occurrence to mention.

"It's about bloody time you came and reported," Bowdler says in welcome as Roger walks into his office. "I'm told you've spent a hell of a lot of money in foreign places. Better have been worth it. What's the story, then?" He points to a seat.

"Actually, I need more money," Roger says coolly. And before Bowdler manages to stoke his irritation into a rant, "It's the immigration story and the lack of checks on who's been let in. You wanted a psychopath; we may have found a really good one."

Bowdler visibly relaxes and motions for Roger to continue.

"It looks like we let in a Cambodian war criminal, a genocidal maniac."

"Cambodia? Who is he and what's he supposed to have done there and, more importantly, here?"

"His name is Khieu and he's wanted, or rather he was wanted, and not very enthusiastically at that, for torture and murder; his speciality was killing children. We have a hunch that he's now in this country. He may be my neighbour, actually."

Bowdler laughs. "I thought you lived among the gentry, Roger, with that whopping salary we pay you. Not next door to Cambodian war criminals."

"Well, it's only a hunch ..."

"A bloody expensive hunch ..."

"But we're paid for our instincts, too, aren't we?" And, before Bowdler gets a chance to suggest where Roger can put his costly *instincts*, "After all, it's your fantastic nose for a story that put you behind that desk, isn't it, chief? I could talk all afternoon about the legendary scoops and exclusives you've got for the paper because of your extraordinary sixth-sense for these things. Everyone has a dirty secret, remember? And there's no one on earth who can see through people better than you."

Lest you think that my boy is indulging in mere flattery and obsequiousness, he's probably right. It's uncanny sometimes how Bowdler can sniff out rot, decay and debauchery in even the most apparently innocent lives. He *assumes* everyone is putrescent and will thus sooner or later commit foul and reprehensible acts (if they haven't done so already, of course). Those acts considered such in nice society, at least, which is the *target audience* of the 'Hack', though that obscene marketing and sales expression has been known to send the man into an apoplectic fit when the promotions boys use it provocatively (deliberately so) at meetings into which the publisher occasionally drags him kicking and screaming.

And Bowdler himself? Where would he place in the depravity stakes? It would be convenient to think that like J. Edgar Hoover he has a secret life while relentlessly condemning and persecuting those who share his particular proclivities, of whatever nature they might be. But there is no evidence nor rumour that this is so. All who have asked themselves the question (and even put a man or two *on the job*, for future exploitation, perhaps, just in case that might one day be necessary and provide a certain protection), have concluded that he is what he appears to be: a cruel, foul-mouthed, uncharitable, morally bankrupt, unethical, shameless, degenerate ogre. He is nevertheless a family man, not known to drink nor smoke nor gamble, who avoids like the plague all the film and theatre premieres, cocktail parties and society dinners to which he is invited, and has never been seen to dally with the many pretty young ladies, or young men, for that matter, who swan around the 'Hack'. Though corrupt in his soul, he is said to be incorruptible in matters of money and favours. He is even rumoured to go to church on Sundays. Oh yes, dear reader, it is difficult sometimes to pigeon-hole a man, most particularly when he doesn't share your own sinful inclinations and desires and yet is quite evidently far less virtuous than you believe yourself to be. And perhaps, after all, Bowdler expends all his propensities for doing harm to the human race through the heinous 'Daily Hack' and simply has no energy left over to further spread evil when he leaves the office? Only one thing is sure, he'll end up a knight or lord of the realm either way for his *services to the nation*. This is how things function in our little country if we are in the good graces of our paymasters. And what an immense joke that will be, ladies and gentlemen, you must agree!

"What's our *angle* on all this?" asks Bowdler. "Supposing you do manage, at great expense, to prove that this chap is who you think he might be—even if, if I've understood correctly, he hasn't even been convicted of anything. We can't run much of a story about the failure to properly check the backgrounds of rich immigrants on the basis of a single, as yet unproven, case. We'd need dozens of them. That could take months to establish, couldn't it? It doesn't look like a good investment of our resources to *me*."

"Perhaps that's so," concedes Roger. "But it's a really important *human rights* story. This man, maybe countless others hidden in our provincial backwaters, is an abject torturer and killer of men, women and children. Surely he has to be exposed, brought to justice, not left to cultivate his garden as though nothing had happened? What hope is there for any of us if we let such things go?"

"Human rights? Since when were you interested in human rights, Roger? Is it a new hobby, or something? Tip off those anarchists at Amnesty if you really want to get this off your chest, but it's not the business of our newspaper to right wrongs in some obscure country half way round the other side of the world. Our readers want us to campaign about the price of chickens—did you see that they're up 16%?—not alleged war crimes in distant places committed before most of them were born. I don't need to teach you any of this, Roger, you know better than any of my reporters what makes our readers tick. That's one of your unique talents."

"Do you know why people were killed in the genocide?" asks Roger.

Bowdler shrugs.

"Because they wore glasses, knew a foreign language, laughed or cried, or expressed love for another person."

"That's original," says Bowdler drily.

"Two million of them, at least. Perhaps three. For absolutely nothing! And our guy was smashing babies heads against trees, when he wasn't raping their mothers or torturing their fathers."

Roger has got very emotional. I encourage him to stay cool and remind him that Bowdler is singularly unmoved by such matters, which remain completely abstract to him, as they do, in fairness, to most people, and especially the 'Hack' readers. He ignores me, perhaps doesn't even hear my appeals to remain detached and lucid if he wants any chance at all of swaying Bowdler.

"Why didn't his own country take care of him?" asks the chief. "Rather than letting him make a fortune and come and spend it here, which can only be good for us. That's how things should work. It's really not our business to go round cleaning up for the others."

Roger thinks of our own and our allies disgraceful conduct after the last world war, facilitating the release and escape, or even hiring, of thousands of German criminals because it was judged expedient for us in some grand geopolitical scheme. He is sure that Bowdler would have argued for that too, putting pragmatism above righteousness, as such men and many others do. If they are not personally involved, of course, which invariably changes everything. For myself, I believe there is no greater good than justice for men here and now and always and I hope that I am gradually persuading our Roger to see things this way too and to act on them in consequence.

"So you really don't care if we're harbouring a genocidal psychopath in my village?" asks Roger boldly. "You'd rather I wrote about starlets having secret boob jobs, would you?"

"On balance, yes I would," says Bowdler coldly. "Though they'd have to be big. The starlets, that is, not the boobs."

"It's a bloody disgrace," says Roger unadvisedly. "It's sickening that the 'Hack' doesn't care about such things."

Bowdler is not at all used to having his views and decisions challenged or hearing derogatory remarks about his precious journal from one of his own reporters and is clearly restraining himself from an explosion of his customary rage.

"You have my verdict, young man. I don't want a penny more spent on this obscure tale you have largely dreamt up if I can judge from the facts you've actually been able to give me. Get back to your real job of uncovering shit and hope in *this* country, shit and hope that affect our readers in their daily lives. That's what they want and that's what we're bloody well going to give them. I don't want to hear another word about your fucking Cambodian. And if you don't like it, go and work for those leftie tossers at the Grauniad; they'd lap it up, I'm sure."

Roger stands, turns and walks out of the office without a word, though with thoughts of murder that I perhaps should not normally mention and indeed would not if his goose were not doubtless already cooked by now on that score and I could not do him any more harm in these pages.

It's not your fault, I tell the boy as he heads for 'The Philistine' (our favourite tavernkeeper has actually changed the name of his establishment, much to Roger's astonishment, on the basis, as he puts it, that he hasn't seen a lion in the place, much less a red one, for years, and that the new name not only is more fitting for the general mood of the place but has proved a roaring success with the customers, proud as they are, in keeping with the whole nation, with this very apt moniker).

How come, Roger asks me? I think I've been very stupid to assume for an instant that the 'Hack' could actually care about such a trivial matter as the murder of three million people.

Remember, though, I tell him, that Bowdler actually accepted your premises at the outset. He didn't make any objection at all to your investigation when you first put it to him. He was even quite enthusiastic. You can hardly blame yourself that he has reverted to type. Perhaps he was distracted the first time. Or, more likely, he's had a royal bollocking from the publisher and the owner about the falling sales and subscriptions. He's never been especially coherent and consistent in what he wants as stories and has simply fallen back on his tired mantras about our readers' ephemeral tastes and preoccupations. Which are currently about the price of chickens, it appears.

I bet he's completely forgotten Syria, Archie and the biological weapons too, Roger suggests.

Yup. I'd also drop that one, if I were you.

I'm not dropping either, Roger tells me, without further explanation.

The lady almost rumbles me!

We left Roger making a flippant proposal of marriage to Sandra in a restaurant, you may remember. She ignored it, of course, as any self-respecting woman would do in the circumstances, though with a deliciously playful laugh.

Perversely, our Roger is rather distressed by her composure. He has just laid his miserable life on the table for dissection, avowed his worthless, practically criminal nature, humiliated and condemned himself, and she continues to sit there as though they are discussing an abstract question of only mild interest to her. He turns to me to make some kind of sense of it all for him.

So, I ask him, what were you expecting or hoping for? To provoke her anger? To be vilified and spat upon? To wallow complacently in your disgrace and her disgust in you? Were you actually looking forward to your crucifixion? Hoping to be cleansed of sin? Perhaps you are giving yourself too much importance, my boy. You are nobody in particular for her, just a Philistine inviting her to a nice lunch. She is not to know how much anguish you have been through to reveal to yourself the vacuity and meaninglessness of your existence. Though she might well be clever enough to suspect it when she thinks all this over on another day. If she can be bothered … Haha!

Roger is actually happy with my little speech. He is beginning to like these brief moments of reprieve from his passionate and emotional excesses. What would the lad do without me? He is even starting to wonder about that himself.

But, in any case, this is how their first proper conversation continued …

"Tell me about yourself, if you would, that is," says Roger. "Is it your own bookshop that I stumbled into?"

"I own it with a friend. We bought it last year. The old shop, where I've been buying books since I was a child, closed down a year before that. It was the last one for miles around. Brigitte—that's my friend—and I weren't doing very much at the time, just odd jobs here and there, so we decided to scramble up some money, mainly by begging our families, who aren't short of a few thousand, and there it is. We're immensely proud of it. Don't you think that a town centre without a bookshop is simply tragic?"

"I could easily be persuaded of it," Roger smiles. "Up until quite recently, I've not given bookshops much of a thought. Not because I was getting books online or anything; I simply haven't been reading all these years. All that is changing, though. I've decided to get myself a culture."

"You've come to the right place then," says Sandra. "We'll have you up and running in no time. Go for quality, not quantity, though. Ten truly great books read well are worth skipping through a thousand poor ones—and God knows there's no shortage of those about these days, though not in our shop, I must say. We chiefly sell the classics. This is perhaps not the best way to make money and be successful, but our aims in that respect are really very modest. Keeping the business above water is about our only ambition."

"You're doing it for the love of literature, then?"

"Yes, if you like. But also because I believe passionately that no life can possibly be rich and fulfilled without the constant stimulation of the arts. Perhaps you have come to the same conclusion, from what you say. But let me ask *you* a question: How do you think to reconcile your new encounters with great ideas and thoughts and truths and perceptions—for, after all, this is what the outstanding writers strive to reveal and illustrate—while working for that monstrous, villainous rag, your 'Hack'? Or are there two Roger P.s?"

Bloody hell, thinks Roger, she's onto us! We have a good, quiet laugh about that, me and the boy.

"I'm going to have to figure that out, it's clear," Roger responds. "I've begun already, of course. Coming into your bookshop was not only a beginning of sorts, or so it appears, it was also the culmination of a very long and painful process of self-examination and reflection."

"It seems that Herr Böll's timing was perfect," Sandra laughs. "It would also confirm something that Albert Camus wrote, about how we always encounter the books we need in our lives at the precise moment we need them. I can't remember the exact quote, but it does often feel exactly like that, even though it's doubtless an illusion."

"What books do I need next, in your opinion?" asks Roger.

"I haven't the faintest idea, of course! As I mentioned when we first met, it's absolutely pointless to recommend books to people when you don't know them intimately. You could do worse than read Camus himself, though, now I think about it. 'The Fall' could be appropriate as a start. You might even find certain parallels between the dilemmas with which you are apparently wrestling and those of the novel's hero, an admired, respected, honoured, fêted—and self-satisfied—lawyer whose inner voice, if I can so describe it, eventually revolts and reveals to him his hypocrisy and mediocrity and complete lack of honour and regard for the truth."

Any resemblance to persons living or dead is purely coincidental, I whisper to Roger.

"Yes, indeed, something of this might ring a bell to me," he says, with a charming, wry smile.

"Of course, the novel has many other themes," adds Sandra. "This is just the framework on which the author hangs his ideas."

"And how does it end for him, this self-disgraced lawyer?"

"That, I shall not tell you. You must read the book for yourself. In any case, we could also well argue that you are going in the opposite direction. From disgrace to honour, no?"

"Do you think that's possible? The only thing I know to do is to be a reporter. I have no knowledge or qualifications for anything at all else in the world. I did, by the way, once write a detective novel, but I suppose it was rubbish because I didn't hear back from a single agent or publisher I sent it to."

'Who knows?" says Sandra. "People are writing books in their millions; a mass of good books must never even see the light of day. In any case, what are we going to do about you, indeed?"

Don't you think it unusual, dear reader, that these two people, who have now had no more than an hour together in their lives, should already share such complicity? Where others, even after ten thousand hours in each other's company, might not even once have approached their level of intimacy? Yet it is so and is truly one of the delightful mysteries of human relations. It seems to me that they have wantonly, wilfully, abandoned already all the barriers we carefully construct to protect and hide ourselves from the others, for fear … of what? Anyhow, enough of these elucubrations. For the conversation takes an even more interesting turn at this moment.

Since Roger is, for once, lost for words, and has no ready reply to Sandra's question, she continues herself.

"If you truly are no good for anything else, we'll have to think of ways you can help from within."

"Help? Help who?"

"How about the human race, my dear? That's a good place to start, isn't it?"

That 'my dear' is so natural, so in tone with their yet unspoken affection, that it surprises neither of them.

"Of course," Sandra continues, "you probably can't be open about it; you must do it surreptitiously, at first."

Roger laughs heartedly. He is so in love. The idea suddenly occurs to him that he has finally met another passionate person and that this is what has been missing in his life. There are fewer of these people around than one might suppose, for better or for worse — depending on what they're up to, of course.

"I'll be an enemy of the interior, the fifth column—very appropriate for a newspaper, don't you think?"

A new dish has arrived and they set about eating it with enthusiasm. Roger is sneaking glances at Sandra from under his lowered eyebrows, hoping to find signs of amorous longings in her face too, as there must be in his, he believes. He sees nothing other than the very pleasant and kindly expression she seems to carry with her everywhere.

"So," says Roger as they sigh with satisfaction at the outstanding crab-stuffed sole with lobster cream sauce that they have both now finished, "how can the human condition be improved in our nation. What needs to be done?"

"I think the people of this country are completely broken and lost, don't you?"

"To be honest, I've not thought much about it," says Roger humbly.

"Yes, it could take a century to repair them," Sandra continues. "Culturally, *spiritually*, if you like, intellectually for sure. We are now attached to nothing at all, except the multitude who still desperately cling to their miserable nostalgia for empire and past greatness. We are completely bankrupt of ideas; we've no dream, no vision, no future in sight. We simply limp from one crisis to another. At the same time, all our traditions, which are so necessary to anchor us to the foundations of our humanity, have been lost and buried. Except for the bloody Morris Dancers, perhaps, who seem to be the only act in town. If you'll excuse my French. I don't swear much, but I can get quite carried away when talking about how this country has gone to the dogs."

Roger has never heard 'bloody' said so beautifully. He yearns to hear it again one day.

"So, if this country has already gone down the tubes, what's to be done?"

"That's the important question," says Sandra. "Personally, I feel useless here, so I give all my spare time and attention to helping people in those countries which are still *becoming* rather than wasting my time and energy on a people like us in inexorable decline. It's every man for himself here and they can well get on with that without *me*."

"Where do newspapers like mine fit into the picture?" asks Roger. "In your view, that is. Wouldn't you say that we were only a reflection of the people, of our readers? If we weren't, I'm not sure why so many millions of them would read us."

"It's because they simply know no better, I should think. They have been fed all your nonsense, trivia, hysteria, trash, crudeness, for so long, at least two generations, that they simply cannot imagine anything else, cannot see beyond your narrow tabloid mindset. Of course, countless people hate you, hate most particularly the 'Hack', but they do so not because you are brainless, soulless, amoral scum—please excuse that word, my dear, it's not personal—but uniquely because of your politics, your blind support, even in the face of corruption or the greatest travesties wrought by their policies, of your ideological masters."

"This is a lot for one day," Roger laughs.

"I see it hasn't spoilt your appetite," says Sandra, pointing at Roger's empty plate. "It was absolutely delicious, though, thanks so much."

"Look, I know you have to go soon and get back to the

shop," says Roger. "But we really have to continue this conversation. I want to hear much more about your activities and concerns about the world outside our lost island, as you describe it."

And they left it there for the day and said fond goodbyes. Now that Roger has Sandra's telephone number, she will hear from him rather rapidly, as you may well imagine. They have a lot of ideas to discuss, not to mention feelings to be explored, and if you are not a complete blockhead, dear reader, you might just be interested to hear about them.

Archie shows an interest in sex

Roger has decided, for better or worse, to confront Archie directly about Baker and the Assad picture. He wants no distraction or diversion, so proposes that the two men go alone for a drink after they have each completed their day's work.

'The Philistine' is no place for a quiet conversation, so Roger chooses an inn by the river bordering their village. Archie is already there and sitting with a drink when he arrives.

"You like this place too, then?" says Archie. "Sheila and I come here quite often for a peaceful moment."

"We don't get here much. I'm generally to be found at one drinking hole or another in town. But this seemed convenient for both of us and it's indeed quite congenial, I agree."

I am witness that Roger has thought out in advance his whole stratagem for getting Archie to squeal. On the basis of what I've seen over the years, he could probably be a fine chess player if he ever took the time to learn the game.

"Cheers, Archie," says Roger touching glasses. "I enjoyed our discussion the other week at your place—Sandra asked me to renew her thanks to you and Sheila for the very fine dinner—and thought that we might pursue it a little. Aside from my actual work, I'm absolutely fascinated by other people's jobs." This is a lie. He's never given a hoot for how the others live and earn their keep. Unless, of course, they're screwing the taxpayer and their political sympathies are, let's say, misguided.

"My work is very dull, especially compared with your exciting and glamorous life," says Archie. "I actually buy your paper—and look out for your stories, of course. You seem to be having a whale of a time, between tête-à-têtes with footballers' wives, jetting about with pretty actresses and rubbing shoulders with gangsters and royalty."

"A lot of what I do is sordid too, Archie," says Roger, uncharacteristically demeaning himself to a relative stranger. Perhaps he's instinctively trying to win the man's confidence. He knows what he's doing, anyhow, of that I am sure, after years of observing him extract secrets and even confessions out of the most unlikely patsies. He really appears as a most charming fellow, Roger; perhaps I haven't insisted enough on this feature of the man. Inside, he may be in turmoil from a cocktail of torments and emotions of one kind or another—and people hate to see the emotions of others, of course, in simple day-to-day life, at least—but outwardly he never appears as anything but calm and kind and, I have to say, very likeable. Such a demeanour is a considerable advantage in life with the others, however unhappy one may be within. But many people, mostly men it seems to me, can keep up this pretty front with ease. It's often even the case of those who do terrible things, to themselves or to the others, after years being considered as model, balanced members of the community. There is some brain organization or other in such lucky souls that separates entirely their emotions and instincts and their intellectual existence. Anyhow, I was recounting a conversation before these idle thoughts waylaid me, wasn't I?

"I can imagine," says Archie kindly. "Crime and violence, two of your paper's specialities, are rarely attractive, of course, however much our entertainment industry makes them appear."

"Indeed. Some days I wish we could stick uniquely to stories about sex. You have no idea, Archie, how popular they are. One of the advantages of the internet for *our* business is that we know exactly who's reading what, how many of them. In the print-only days, that was always a hit and miss affair; we largely had to guess what people liked. Now, we have the figures. And, as it ever was, I suppose, it's sex that gains all the attention, it's sex that sells. I swear we can announce that half the country will disappear into the sea by the end of next week, or that a meteorite will devastate the south on Saturday, or that Russia has just invaded Germany, still it is that the most read article will remain, by a long way, 'Minister Filmed Groping Secretary, Says He's *In Love*'."

Sex is clearly a subject which interests Archie. He even has thoughts about it.

"It's amazing that in our supposedly liberated country, people are so obsessed still with other people's sex lives, isn't it?" he ventures.

"Takes their minds off chemtrails," says Roger.

Archie laughs. "But this obsession surely should be a story in itself, shouldn't it, Roger? I rarely if ever see it treated that way, though."

"You have a good point, I have to say. But it's a story that will never be written. Not at the 'Hack', at least, if anywhere. We absolutely have to maintain the illusion that it's the *others* who are doing all the illicit shagging in the country. If we let on that our own readers are doubtless far worse philanderers than even government ministers, or more often than not simply frustrated that they're stuck in lives where this isn't possible and where they can only dream of it, what would we do with our righteous indignation over the sexual corruption of our masters? The bottom would go out of our business!

So we're sticking to our voyeuristic infatuation with the sex lives of others. And chasing chemtrails instead."

"You didn't do a piece on that after all, did you, though? I couldn't find anything on the 'Hack's' site, in any case."

"We're not ready yet. We're still investigating."

"Really? What more is there to know?"

"Well, perhaps it's just idle curiosity, but one thing led to another and we started looking into biological warfare. Not only because of that forgotten story about our forty years of self-poisoning, but because there are accusations and rumours about intentions in this respect in the Ukraine conflict. We want to be ready if anything were actually to happen there. Despite appearances, we do on the whole like to know what we're talking about. Perhaps you could help us, actually, as an expert?" Roger slips in, clever fellow. He is watching Archie very closely and suspects he sees a cloud pass over the man's otherwise clear eyes ...

"You know I can't talk about these things," says Archie pleasantly after a moment's pause.

"Of course. You told me that certain things were off limits, but I assumed that you only meant things that you and your Institute colleagues were working on yourselves. That doesn't include biological weapons, surely? But would you like another beer? I'll get them." And my boy wanders off to the bar without waiting for a response. Very neat one there, I tell him as he waves to get the barman's attention. Let's see how our biochemist gets out of *that*.

"Look," Archie starts, before Roger even sits down. "We advise on many issues related to biotechnology. We're a research institute. We assess the pros and cons of this or that technique and the results of their implementation. We have contracts with breweries, for example, or major food companies, who hire us to ensure that they don't accidentally kill their customers with contaminated bread."

"That's very reassuring. But you did also mention that

you worked for the Ministry of Defence and some foreign governments. Not about baking, I assume."

"You mentioned it, actually, not me," says Archie without letting go of his smile. "And you may remember that I said I couldn't discuss such matters, that they were covered by official secrets legislation and confidentiality agreements. I'm afraid that's still the case. I have to be especially careful about this when talking to ace investigation reporters working for the country's largest newspaper, of course."

Roger laughs. "No, no, consider me just as a neighbour and a friend. Of course, I would never use anything you ever said to me in the 'Hack' without your explicit permission." Like hell you wouldn't, I whisper to my honourable friend …

"Anyhow, I suppose that the chemtrails of the summer will soon disappear into the mists of autumn, so you'll get less heat on that one," Archie suggests.

"Indeed, indeed. But Ukraine and all the wild threats from the Kremlin aren't about to go away, of course. Nor the endless strife and fighting in Syria, where chemical weapons are being used on a regular basis, I understand." Roger believes he sees another cloud come over the amiable look from Archie's fine blue eyes. "Ever been to Syria, Archie?"

"Don't insist, please, Roger. I'm completely firm on our principles about confidentiality, you know."

"Quite, quite," says Roger. "Well, I guess I'd better be getting home. Sandra doesn't see enough of me as it is, without me hanging around taverns well beyond the working day or night. It's been nice to have this chat, Archie. We must really keep in touch more regularly. I know we don't live far from each other, but perhaps we could become 'friends' on Facebook, like the youngsters do!"

"Facebook? I'm not on Facebook," says Archie. "I'm much too busy for that. I believe that Sheila has a 'page'—that's what you call it, isn't it? Or a 'profile', or something or other. Perhaps you could look her up; I've never bothered, nor do I intend to. We must keep parts of our lives separate, even in the best of marriages, don't you think?"

"I couldn't agree more," Roger concludes, as they get up and leave. "See you soon."

Roger and the state of grace

"Did you have a nice time? I wouldn't have thought that Archie was exactly your type, but I guess you must have some life outside the home and the office," says Sandra sympathetically. "Unless, of course, you were still working ..." she smiles. "Indulging your suspicious nature about everything and everybody. What did you talk about, anyhow? I imagine you've exhausted those airplane stories by now."

"Sex, mainly," says Roger, plonking himself down in an armchair next to his drinking cabinet, from which he simultaneously extracts a whisky bottle and glass.

"You men!"

"Nothing personal. Men hardly ever discuss sex together, in my experience, and contrary to what many women appear to think. Sex, rather, as a societal and journalistic phenomenon. And as our national obsession, of course."

Sandra laughs. "And what did you conclude from this very academic discussion, my husband?"

"Nothing much, though Archie made an interesting point. He said we spend all our time talking about sex, not only my paper, but the qualities too—though they do it rather more pompously—but we rarely if ever talk about why we are always talking about it. If we dared to, I think we might come up with some rather interesting conclusions."

"Such as?"

"That despite all the undoubted libertinage—or is it libertinism?—going on overtly or covertly in the country, great swathes of the population are fundamentally frustrated, sexually frustrated. How else could one possibly explain why we're constantly writing and talking about it? How could anyone with a fulfilling sex life ever be arsed to care what other people are up to in the matter? We can't forever go on blaming the moral straightjackets with which we were supposedly bound a hundred years ago, can we?"

Roger looks up from the depths of his whisky and finds the room empty. He laughs to himself. When he goes on a bit in this way, Sandra often wanders off to do other things and leaves him talking alone. When they first married, this drove him crazy—how dare she show such lack of interest or respect for him? Now, he loves her beyond words for her occasional lack of curiosity in what he is saying and her lack of endeavour to hide it. You see, dear reader, he is a happy, confident and satisfied man these days. He doesn't need a permanent audience or the approval of the others, as he has invariably done in his short life up until now. He is sufficient finally to himself, perhaps? And if and when a man does reach this state of grace, he can count himself lucky indeed. I like to think that I am not foreign to this happy evolution.

When Sandra returns, telling him to set the table for dinner, he asks if she could do something for him later—have a look on Facebook and track down the page or profile of Sheila Samuels.

Over their meal, Sandra asks: "So why are you interested in Sheila all of a sudden?"

"It's a long story. But what do you know about her, if anything?"

"Very little, actually. She did tell me that she met Archie while both were working at the Institute. For several years she was the secretary of his predecessor, apparently. What was the name?"

"Baker. He gave his name to the Institute itself. Archie's now chief honcho in his place."

"Apart from that, I know nothing, apart from the fact she's biological." They laugh. "She did say that she'd stopped working after Archie got the top job, though, and implied that they no longer needed the money."

"I can believe it, judging from their house. It was impressive, don't you think?"

"Yes, I do. A lot of money came from somewhere or other, because I doubt they could acquire it on the salary of a research institute director, frankly."

"Let's not gossip about that, though," says Roger.

"That's rich from the King of Gossip!" laughs Sandra. "Anyhow, as we were talking I was looking for Sheila, as you asked. No trace of her name on Facebook, I'm afraid. What's this all about, anyhow?"

"I want to show you something. Do a search for the name, what was it ... yes, Utagho, U-t-a-g-h-o ..."

"Got it. No profile information ... nothing recent at all in the way of posts ... a bunch of pictures of grey men in meetings ... all from several years ago, it seems. Why does this interest you, though?"

"This 'Herbert E. Baker' to which this page is dedicated, is *our* Baker, the man who founded Archie's institute, his predecessor and, I now learn from you, Sheila Samuels' former boss too. I don't know what all that adds up to, if anything, though."

"Nor I. Principally because you haven't told me what you're working on, what you *suspect*, if anything."

"Show me the page again. Scroll through the photos, if you would. Stop there. Do you recognize anyone? Goofy, for example?"

"Of course, that's Al-Assad, the Syrian tyrant."

"Indeed. And the short man hanging on to his hand? That's Herbert E. Baker."

"And the fellow over in the corner, half hidden?" asks Sandra.

"No, it couldn't be."

"Yes it is. I'd swear to it. It's our Archie."

"Good grief. I didn't notice that. Our boys don't know Archie from Adam, so they wouldn't have mentioned it, either. The plot thickens."

"Whatever the plot may be."

"So Archie's been frequenting these sons of bitches, too. The guys in the other pictures don't look very pretty, either, do they?" says Roger, pointing at various surly, swarthy men in military uniform. "I doubt whether they're discussing bread-making, frankly."

"I beg your pardon?"

"Archie gave baking techniques to me as an example of what he works on. Protecting us all from poisonous loaves."

"I see."

So what *is* all this about? Roger asks me, since Sandra has wandered off again. Who would think to put up such incriminating photos on a page of remembrance? We know they were taken from Baker's study by Archie, but what could he possibly gain from their publication? He doesn't actually want anyone to see them, does he, otherwise he wouldn't deny any activity or knowledge of Facebook? That only leaves Sheila, of course, who is on Facebook—Archie said so —but not under her name. And who or what or where is Utagho?

"Does Utagho mean anything to *you,* darling?" Roger asks the reappearing Sandra. "It's not the capital of Burkina Faso or something is it?"

Sandra laughs. "No, my dear. That's Ouagadougu. Don't parade your ignorance. It's not your most attractive characteristic, you know. Except at 'The Philistine', I suppose. Do you still go there, by the way?"

"I do occasionally, yes. For old time's sake. It's where I began to make the acquaintance of a certain Mr *Boell,* shortly after meeting the woman of my life for the first time. As you may remember. Anyhow, my love, I have an idea: Why don't you invite Sheila over for a cup of coffee, or something, one day? She can't be very occupied and may appreciate a chat while the men are out in the world. With all your guile, you might get something out of her."

"Since when did you put me on your payroll, Mister Investigations Editor?" asks Sandra with mock indignation. "But why not, after all, if you will first bring me up to date with the story so far. Perhaps I might even be able to stop you from making some awful mistake or other. Yes, I'll ask her over on one of my afternoons off from the shop. And report back to my new boss."

"Thanks a lot, my love. I'll tell you everything we know later. For the moment, I have to make a few phone calls."

As he gets up to go to his study, Sandra says: "Ghouta."

"Pardon?"

"Ghouta. Utagho is an anagram of Ghouta."

"And Ghouta? What's that?"

"It's the suburb of Damascus where the Syrian army killed over a thousand people in a sarin attack. Don't you remember? Those heart-wrenching photos of small children gassed to death in their homes and streets?"

"Good God, yes, that's it. You're a remarkably clever girl, you know."

"Yes, I know," Sandra smiles. "I just never talk about it. That's another sign of my intelligence, of course."

Roger gets a bone to pick

One afternoon, Marjorie calls Roger and says that Bill, the photographer, has come up with something that might be of interest. Would he mind seeing him?

The big, burly Bill, for once without his camera equipment strapped to or hanging from every available part of his body, as Roger usually sees him rushing into and out of the building, knocking everybody aside, is holding a large bone as he enters the office.

"Thanks, but I've had lunch," Roger tells him. Bill grunts. He is a man with a purpose and seems rarely to listen to what people say, even if technically he clearly does hear them. He doesn't seem to grasp the meaning of their words, as it were, in his world of pictures.

Bill puts the bone down on Roger's desk and just stands there.

"Thanks, Bill, but I told Marjorie that I really didn't want to take it back. I'd toss it away or give it to another dog if I were you."

Bill smiles and says: "It's a human bone. A human leg bone."

Roger looks at it and asks: "How do you know? From what I can see, it could as well be a horse. What makes you so sure?"

"It's a human bone," Bill repeats. "A kid, actually, or probably. Might at a pinch be a small woman, also."

"You know your bones then, Bill? Bill the Bone Man."

Bill doesn't take this badly, because he doesn't register this mockery, it seems, just goes on.

"I have this mate who's a doctor. He was round at my place having a drink and spotted the bone on my sideboard. He said he didn't know whether to call the police to arrest me, or what, but it was a human bone, likely a child. He had no doubt at all. I spun him a yarn about why I had it in my possession. I don't think he understood a word I said; not sure I did either."

"How very odd," says Roger. "What would my neighbour's dog be doing with a human bone?"

"Don't know. But I thought you should have it. I don't want human bones lying around my sitting room. And I thought it might help your story, whatever it is. I'd like to work more for you, you know. I'm tired of snatching tit and bum shots of half-naked actresses at premieres, you know. I'd really like to be in on investigations. My late dad was a detective sergeant, you know. Got shot, sadly."

"You've done the right thing, Bill, bringing the bone to me. Good instinct. I'll have one of my team call you soon about doing some of our jobs."

Bill beams and thanks him and leaves. Roger remains at his desk poking and staring at the bone and, with my help, putting 2 and 2s together …

A Playful Examination of Important Psychological Matters

Truths that carry the potential to wound and perhaps even eventually to change people must be told to them at exactly the right time, in the right circumstances—and in the right manner, of course; that is, with respect—if they are to be beneficial and not rejected out of hand, nor earn their authors a barrage of insults or perhaps a punch on the nose. Judging when the conditions are favourable for such truths to be, if not especially welcomed by, at least useful to their recipients, requires a high degree of psychological insight.

Unhappily, though men are to a certain extent capable of acquiring this insight, it remains one of the poorest and least evolved in their mental arsenals. One does not, alas, develop psychological acuity from the study of theories at university, which has proven quite useless for uncovering any profound perceptions about the functioning of the human mind, as we have all been able to see for ourselves if we've met or otherwise encountered a professional psychologist or two, particularly those of the cognitive variety (which is the only one that really interests Roger). Indeed, if we are to judge from the unspeakable trivia produced by the research centres of psychology's academia, the experts remain stuck in the stone age of thought's mechanics, still light years behind what has already been understood by our greatest novelists and the occasional philosopher.

Such is the depth of society's failure to identify and clarify anything significant about men's minds, it has been known to grasp at straws. All the Dunnings and Krugers in the world may impress our pop culture with their trifling 'discoveries' of the blindingly obvious and unhidden, may announce with great fanfare that stupid and ignorant people on the whole don't know how stupid and ignorant they are, and that intelligent and well-informed people, on the other hand, underestimate themselves, still it is that Socrates, for one, told us precisely that two and half thousand years ago and that it's perhaps time to move on to a higher level of understanding.

Yes, my dear reader, we have been reading our Plato! I have it here. The enlightened prison authorities, bless them, allow Roger to have as many books as he can buy and fit into his cell (his co-detainees, alas, have all rather opted for television sets …) and none is far from his reach. Yes, here it is. Roger has underlined countless passages and scrawled his own remarks in the margins, most notably this: 'He who knew nothing and knew that he knew nothing was declared by the oracle the wisest of men. The others, who knew little or nothing, imagined they knew all things …' Perhaps Roger sees here a parallel to his own case?

The really funny thing in the case of the much flaunted Dunning-Kruger 'effect' is that the research on which it is based was carried out on students of psychology; that, ladies and gentlemen, well justifies the dearth of hope we might have for the immediate future of the discipline. Not to mention, of course, that anyone who believes even for an instant that a small group of American juveniles (not to pick especially on our transatlantic friends, of course; youth is youth and ignorant everywhere) would possess the self-awareness and intellectual maturity to judge themselves and their perceptions and knowledge coldly, in an objective manner, if you like, and be capable of adapting their positions in the face of contradiction, deserves to be force-fed as much of this mind fodder as the universities and the media can churn out for their consumption.

If the researchers were not so busy confirming what can be observed by and is already obvious to a bright five-year-old child, they might start examining something much more interesting and useful to humanity: *How* can we nurture men like Socrates, men who have realistic opinions about themselves and their knowledge and their flaws and their limitations? Men who would put truth and justice above even their personal desires, instincts and interests? What is the obstacle to the development of such men? Surely it is not that trifling phenomenon which in a rather laboured manner the psychologists describe as *cognitive bias*, a term that has most regrettably escaped the mind laboratories and entered into common vocabulary and is so bandied about in the media and on social networks—generally by people who prefer to pin a label on you rather than an argument—that a man might easily suffer nausea from once more hearing it.

I should tell you that in addition to most of Plato, Roger has now read practically all the works of Albert Camus, the wisest of the thinkers of our age. Sandra is a true *aficionada* of the writer and my boy's ambition is to discover for himself as many of the authors she loves as he can manage. Though he knows he will never catch up with her—she is a truly voracious reader—it gives them more and more thoughts and ideas to share and discuss together.

It is in Camus that Roger has found the most striking thought about philosophy that he ever encountered: "There is only one really serious philosophical problem," Camus contends, "and that is suicide. Deciding whether or not life is worth living is to answer the fundamental question in philosophy. All other questions follow from that."

Well, dear reader, to cut a long story short (we'd certainly appreciate *that*, do I hear you say?), I've been wondering if perhaps one might venture a fundamental thought of such magnitude also in the matter of psychology and the study of the workings of our delicate and complex human minds. What else do I have to do with my time, after all, other than to stare at the walls of Roger's cell and ponder such questions? Until the day comes, of course, when we have a little visit to make back out into the great world. But plans for that have already been set and there's no point in going over them all again. You'll hear about them too in time, if only you're patient, don't worry.

So, what in psychology can be said to be above all else in importance? To tell the truth, as I always do, of course (whether you want to believe that or not is your concern and not mine), I know already the 'one serious problem' that is desperately seeking elucidation and could quite well be the foundation of all other matters that we like to consider essential in our explorations of man's mind. It is one that remains absurdly neglected in the general scheme of things, perhaps a little because of semantic confusion, however unfortunate and rather risible that would be if it were indeed the case. This *problem of all problems* faced by psychology is to understand why some men have an inner voice—or perhaps we should call it an eye, or even a whole *persona,* while we're at it—and some men do not. In good Athenian society of old, there was perhaps only a single man of this kind, only a single man who possessed the eye and the voice—he called it, among other things, his 'internal oracle'. Only one who would admit it, at least. Were the others cowards, unwilling to displease the established order? Or were they rather simply *passion's slaves, fools to fortune* (to borrow words from our greatest poet), bereft of the ability to hear and see themselves in a detached manner?

But what can we call this player, in Roger's case your humble servant, of course, who has come forth timidly on the stage of the human mind? I'm sure the Greeks have a word for the phenomenon, the ancients that is. Indeed, Socrates had a good shot at it himself when he spoke of his *daimonion,* the mocking voice within him that 'always deters me from the course of action I was intending to engage in', as he put it. But we don't want to threaten the mental stability of our children with the learning of Greek in our day, more's the pity, so we have lazily adopted the expression 'self-awareness', which is not only all things to every man, of course, but falls critically short of addressing the heart of the matter, the essential question: Is this awareness *just there,* or is it an inescapable ability that man must *develop* to restrain himself from acting on the bidding of his demons? If 'self-awareness' is indeed the foundation of man's capacity to judge, censor, control, prevent his innate criminality from expressing itself, why then is it not the absolute centre of all psychological study without exception? That is the question. (My suspicion that the expression eludes the problem was confirmed once more to me at Roger's trial, when his bumbling attempts to explain himself were met with a cold, "So, you are self-aware?" from the judge. "So what?" this learned gentleman said rather crudely, "Aren't we all?").

Oh for the good old days of penis envy, phallic symbols, the desire to sexually abuse our mothers and kill our fathers, the times when some extravagant and hopefully perverse longings might suddenly pop out of our *unconscious minds* and lead us astray, or at least reveal to us our supposed self-deception and the 'real' truth about what we *actually think* and *truly* want? Haha! Alas, the Freudian hocus pocus with which once upon a time we idly amused ourselves on days out in the country and at dinner parties, those quaintly wicked ideas that dominated public discourse for at least two generations, has now been firmly replaced in the lexicon of the new psychological truths—and thus in the minds of the people—by the upstart *cognitive bias* and its astonishing declensions.

And do you know what? There is no way out of this labyrinth of bias, my friends, if ever you really seek one (and it is an undeniable fact that there are countless people in our societies who actually *desire* to be trapped in a matrix of psychological definitions about themselves; to be told, in short, who they are). Your case is lost before it has even been adequately examined by the jury. For at the instant, the very moment, that you become certain beyond contradiction that you never had any of their five dozen biases, or that you did have some but managed to escape from them, or that you quietly strangled them one by one over the years or even destroyed them in one dramatic blood-drenched bias massacre, perhaps; just when you are ready to declare yourself a free man, a man who judges and decides everything on the basis only of truth, reason and justice, and not at all because of your personal history or bad character, the psychologists will pull out the ace card they've been keeping up their sleeves for just this occasion: We are very sorry, Sir, Madam, but you are completely misled about yourself; we regret to inform you that you are, in fact, an unsuspecting victim of the *Illusion of Objectivity*. Our research proves that your mind is actually unable to become sufficiently detached from your personality in order to judge with any clarity at all your own case and, least of all, your biases. Guilty as charged, next please!

Yes, this is what we have to deal with, my friends, and it is not an easy task by any means, so determined is our opposition that a man might even think that its principal ambition, its whole raison d'être, is to further enchain us rather than to help us in our liberation. Instead of lounging around their mind labs dreaming up the next new *cognitive bias,* pulling ever more tightly the straps on the mental straight-jackets from which they predict we shall never free ourselves, these ladies and gentlemen would do much better to direct their attention toward how we might climb out of the holes they continue to dig for the human race and start constructing the great edifice of enlightenment within which we must plan man's great escape from himself!

Why, you ask, am I so anxious to try and explain these matters to you? Why do I once more lead you off on expeditions into such considerations? You perhaps consider them abstract; don't very much care about them in the general scheme of things? They do not stop you from sleeping at night, do they? Might they, though, if someone was right at this instant planning to fire a missile into your apartment block with the ambition to kill you? Wouldn't that precise moment actually be a good one to ask how on earth the decision to murder you and your neighbours could possibly be taken by men who understood themselves, held themselves to account, and, not least, were aware precisely what they were doing and why they were doing it, in other words killing complete strangers, men, women and children, for no reason at all. We can be sure of one thing: the artillery commander who is just about to end your existence on this earth, surely a victim of his cognitive bias, is certainly not a man of the Socratic school of thought.

But perhaps you are not impressed by the great truths of philosophy or psychology? Perhaps you have not even ever been suicidal, for example? I'm told that such people exist. But whether you personally sympathize or not with my efforts to get a firmer grip on man's mind is absolutely beyond my control and thus perhaps also my interest. All I can tell you is that I am pursuing this endeavour because I do actually care, all jokes aside, about the future of our species and believe beyond contradiction that the keys to peace and prosperity lie in only one location—the inside of the human head. And it is not a question of learning, nor intelligence, nor any especial intellectual prowess. This Socrates about whom I speak with such respect, even love, was truly a simple man who cared little for theories—he claimed not even to read the natural philosophers of his time! But he did ask questions, of the others, of course, and above all of himself, and even occasionally told a story or two …

It goes without saying, of course, that beyond these ambitions to save humanity, on a more modest scale I am trying to help save one man. For if Roger is to survive this whole ordeal, and his life in general, and to do so without undue suffering, he must understand at least what it was all about, don't you believe? I'm sure you know this for yourself: many things may seriously trouble a man's or woman's mind, but the hardest to deal with, the hardest problems to resolve, are as often as not those which we cannot actually articulate or explain to ourselves, those for which we cannot find adequate words to assuage their unbearable pressure. It is so, my friends, however odd, perhaps even paradoxical, it may appear: our very worst mental agonies are often those we are incapable of naming. This alone is sufficient reason to turn to greater minds than our own who have found the words …

There will never be any shortage, of course, of people who will tell you what problem you have when you are unable to do it for yourself. But in regard to the one that should interest us beyond all others, they seem to me to be quite lost. And what is that problem that we cannot admit or even adequately name? It is the titanic struggle which we humans are waging to take control of our minds and thus our deadly, mortifying instincts. We are still fixated on the nature of man's mental aberrations, handicaps and defects, endlessly refining our names for, and theories about, them, but we cannot seem to properly exploit his embryonic capacity for bringing them to heel for his own and the general good.

Still, the gurus shout: You are *wonderful*! But we are not wonderful at all (though it does appear that there are some rare souls who are naturally so; not many, but some.) No, we do not need to erect feeling good about ourselves as some kind of religious totem. Yes, many things will be quite impossible for us all, now and for always. Our positivity gurus are wasting our time, our precious, precious time. To put it in the crudest way possible, to ensure the widest understanding: If you are a shit, like Roger has been for many years, admit it, to yourself at least (little if anything will be gained, and much perhaps lost, by shouting it in Times Square). If you are envious, jealous, racist, hateful, have dreams of murder, destruction, vengeance, or are simply indifferent to the suffering of the others, accept all that, don't try and fool yourself that you are a decent person; you are what you are. Nothing prevents you from getting better with time, but meanwhile your and our only concern is that you not damage the others, that you *do not act* on your most abject instincts. That's all that really counts at the end of the day. No one asked you or even provided the conditions for you to become a saint, so don't let it get you down. Yes, dear reader, if we could only find ways simply to stop people *acting* on their evil and destructive instincts, rather than telling them they don't have any, or endlessly analysing their origin, we could save the world. We need to accept and love one thing only: our remarkable capacity to understand, judge and reason with ourselves.

Our very survival now, today, depends on the most important question in psychology—the counterpoint to Camus on philosophy: "There is only one really serious problem in psychology and that is: How do we teach man to *take sides against* himself?" Every other problem pales in significance in the light of this one and every other question leads away from it.

This particular psychological question didn't matter so much, of course, when we were fighting each other only with bows and arrows and spears, those simpler times when shits were shits and that only mattered if one of them happened to take a dislike to you, or wanted your land or coveted your possessions. In our epoch, half a country can be wiped out, tens perhaps hundreds of thousands killed, on a single man's whim and command. We think, because we've lived a while with this prospect, that it has gone away. Well, dear reader, you must think again as long as men exist in the palaces of power for whom reason, justice and truth are mere abstract concepts to which they owe no personal allegiance at all.

This is why I'm expending an inordinate amount of time and words on the question, while you are only impatient for me to get on with the famous story.

So, where was I with *that* before wandering off on this thought-filled digression? Yes, I was about to tell you about certain truthful matters pertaining to Roger, as presented to him by his wife, Sandra, a psychologist of the first order, in my view, soon after their marriage.

It was the umbrella-on-the-roof incident with which I began this story that finally led to it. Roger's behaviour that sunny day was very much typical of him at the time. Before Sandra, he had never been close to another human being in his life and had not thus realised that along with the great joy that this new relationship brought him, there were certain obligations too. Happily, I was there to help him understand this. Indeed, on the very evening of the rooftop drama, we had a good, healthy discussion about it.

You know you shouldn't have spoken to her like that, don't you boy, I began? Screaming like a man possessed, not because of the dangerous risk you perceived in Sandra's actions (she is, after all, more than capable of judging that for herself); not because she said one thing to you and did another; not, as you so absurdly claimed, because she had *betrayed* you and your trust.

Why then, asked Roger? What actually inspired me to go off the deep end like that? I must have sounded very stupid, I know, but what was it all for?

I did try to intervene, you know, but you shouted me down too.

I really should listen to you more often, I know. Now that I'm convinced you're on my side. But I've always been afraid that if I took all your admonitions seriously, if I eliminated all that in my mind you have revealed as false, you'd finish by emasculating, destroying me, you'd take away so much of my personality that there'd be nothing left, hardly a shadow of a man.

You have far too much passion for that, Roger, I reassure him. This passion will save you, I promise. I am certain of this.

But why do I act as I did? You haven't answered that yet.

You have a natural need or desire for domination, for control, I'd say, the instincts of a baboon chief, really. Not that you require to be obeyed—our democratic age has made this socially unacceptable—but you find it very difficult to handle opposition and contradiction and not to be *in charge*. You want far too much to be *right*. But you must let go of that. Not because one cannot be right more often than not, but because it suffocates other people, becomes unbearable for them, if you insist on it. And what do you gain if you beat them into submission? Nothing at all, nothing whatsoever, nothing except their enmity. Another factor comes to mind: You still want to be the centre of attention, don't you? All those years at school and home where you couldn't find anyone with whom to discuss your existential misgivings, where everyone ignored you, didn't want to hear your opinions. Perhaps you still just want to be loved, as you did back in those days?

That's a lot to think about, Roger tells me. You do realize, though, that I've not been aware that I've been behaving in such a way? That it's not *intentional*, if you like, not deliberate. I don't want or need domination over anyone at all, least of all Sandra. You know I practically *enjoy* it when she contradicts me, shows me that I'm wrong about an awful lot of things.

That's what I'm here for, my boy, that's precisely my assignment—to make you more aware of what you are doing and why it's wrong, so we can have you behave in a manner that actually reflects your good character, of which I don't have much remaining doubt.

Anyhow, two days later, with remarkably good timing, Sandra herself served him another giant helping of humble pie to feast upon. She had not said a word about the umbrella commotion; had let him wilt alone in the great heat of the afternoon sun while she left the house on some errand or other as though nothing had happened. Since she is not greatly given to explanations, as we have noted, Roger thought at the time that she had simply chosen to ignore and hopefully forget his unbecoming behaviour. After all, it was quite meaningless; just words.

Looking back on it, I am once more confounded by the great delicacy of this extraordinary woman. She did not even say, "Roger, we have to talk," or anything of the kind that would have raised his defensive guard in the way such words, dripping with menace, have a tendency to do with those who harbour guilt. She just said, casually, apropos of nothing at all, while they were preparing dinner in the kitchen: "There is little in my life as important to me as words. I have no sympathy whatsoever with those in our generation who increasingly equate correctness in language, in spelling, grammar or, above all, *meaning*, with some insane idea of pretentiousness or elitism. As Camus said so truly: 'To misname things is to add to the misfortune of the world'. You agree with that, don't you, darling?"

"I wish I had read Camus a long time before you introduced him to me, sweetheart. Do you remember—on our first date you suggested I read 'The Fall'? Which I did straight away."

"Yes, I do," Sandra smiles. "In those days, long ago—what was it, six months?—you would have delved passionately into the reading of the 'Instruction Manual of a Hitachi Underfloor Heater-Cooler System' if I'd suggested it were a good thing to do."

Roger laughs heartedly. "I'm sorry, sorry, sorry! I'll do it, I promise you. And in the original Japanese, if you like; I'm sure it's more comprehensible than the English version I've tried to read once or twice and abandoned."

"That would be great, my love. There's a definite autumn chill in the house already and we'll have to get it functioning sooner or later. Or freeze. On this subject of words, though. You used a few the other day in the garden that stayed with me. You didn't mean them, did you?"

"No, my love. I feel so guilty about it all. What I said was completely gratuitous, didn't correspond in the slightest to what I felt, what I feel. I really don't know where it all came from. But I've been thinking about it a lot."

Sandra says nothing. They aren't even looking at each other. She is busying herself cutting potatoes, while he leans against the sink and swirls the drink in his glass.

"I come from a world where we also give great importance to words, you know," he continues. "Not at all in the same way as you, though, not because they hold any value as ways of expressing honest thoughts or feelings or insights or whatever. Words for us on the 'Hack' are only weapons for us to wound or to amuse or to excite hysteria and indignation. We don't really believe them; they're just ... what can I call them ... ideograms, or some such? Just symbols, if you like, intended to imply or provoke a preconceived prejudice. Or something. Am I talking rubbish, darling?"

Sandra laughs gaily. "It was brave attempt, my love, to explain tabloidspeak, in any case."

And there they left it. The umbrella-on-the-roof affair was never spoken of again.

She was Baker's lover

"I've got the story, boss. And what a story it is."

"Marjorie …"

"Marjorie? Who's Marjorie?"

"Sandra! I'm sorry."

"So, who's Marjorie? I thought you'd put your philandering days behind you."

"Sorry, darling! You never call me on the office phone, so I assumed it was one of my team. Marjorie is one of my investigators."

"Hmmm. Tell that to the judge. In any case, since I'm now on the staff, I thought I should pass through official channels. You have an awfully nice receptionist, you know; she didn't hesitate to put me through, though I'm sure all sorts of women are calling you day and night."

Roger wisely doesn't contradict her and asks: "I'm dying to hear it, anyhow. What is the story."

"It seems that Sheila is also married to a miscreant. For love, despite everything. I've been thinking about it. How do they handle it? Eva Braun, Mrs Stalin, there were two of them …"

"Mrs Pol Pot."

"In any case, I haven't got time to gossip about dictators' wives. You'll have to wait until you get home to hear what I've learnt. I have to go out for a bit of shopping now." And with that, Sandra hung up.

Roger went home early, as you may imagine.

"Drinking at five? This is new, Mrs P."

Sandra is sitting at the dining room table with a large glass of gin and tonic.

"I've been through quite an emotional couple of hours today, you know. There's been a lot of sobbing in your house and not only Sheila, I have to say."

"So, what's the story?"

"Right. Sheila was not only Baker's secretary, they were lovers. According to her, they were going to get married when there had been decent lapse of time after his wife's death. She killed herself too, did you know that?"

"No, I didn't. So she committed suicide a year before he does the same thing. The police even speculated that he did so in grief at losing her. His children didn't buy that theory. Seems they were right, since he was shagging his secretary. How long had that been going on, by the way?"

"Several years, she told me. They were really in love, apparently, or at least she was. We'll just have to take her word for it that he felt similarly. But don't use that word 'shagging', Roger, you know I don't like it. Terribly vulgar."

Roger smiles. "Sorry, sweetheart, we don't know how to speak any differently at the office. It'll take me a while to rid myself of all that, you know."

"Anyhow, where was I? Well, I suppose it's a classic story —I'll have to think of a novel that recounts it, the 19th century must be packed with them—but in her distress and heartbreak over losing her 'Herbie', as she called him, she fell straight into the arms of the nearest man. And he, of course, was Archie, who was single like her."

"Very touching," says Roger, who is not of a particularly sentimental disposition.

"So, up to that point, we have a love story, or perhaps even two. And then it gets a little more troubled and a little more interesting. A lot more, actually. I showed Sheila the Facebook page. She completely broke down. Said that when she eventually married Archie, a year after Herbie's death, they moved together into a fine, new big house, the one we know, all the while wondering how they could afford it, since her new husband is not a man ever to talk of money or where his own comes from. It angered him when she once brought it up, so she just dropped the subject and began enjoying the good life. Fill my glass, will you darling."

"Yes, yes, sorry, I should have thought to do it. Get 'em drunk and they'll all talk, we say in the business."

When Roger returns with the drink, she continues without prompting.

"And then one day … she's tidying up Archie's study—they have a cleaning lady, she said, but she can't get out of her old habits as a poor, single girl—and when she's knocking some dust off a framed painting on the wall, it falls and just like in a bad crime novel there's a safe in the wall behind it and, lo and behold, it's open."

"Who could resist that?" says Roger.

"Indeed. And inside, there's a stack of files, some financial accounts, and a pile of photos. Of Herbie, of course, and a couple with Archie in the background. She flicks through the documents, which are in the names of different companies she's never heard of, and the financial papers, which reveal huge sums of money going in and out of bank accounts in distant places well-known as havens for shell companies and dubious goings on. As former secretary to the Institute—whose name isn't mentioned anywhere—she knows her way around paperwork, does Sheila. And it doesn't take her more than a few minutes to figure out that her Archie and her late love Herbie Baker have been up to mischief and secretly making a very handsome packet on the side, because their names appear frequently on the contracts, together with their signatures."

"Fascinating. And does she conclude anything about what they've been up to, on the side?"

"Yes. She does. Baker has scrawled notes here and there. She swears that she is the only person in the world other than him who could actually understand them, after being tortured for years deciphering his handwriting. Here and there he has annotated obscure, one-page contracts that are so expressed that no one could see anything untoward in them, with words like 'sarin compounds', 'technical advice', and, wait for it, 'Ghouta bonus'—this one dated just after the 2013 massacre. By this time, Sheila is weeping in my arms, practically unable to talk comprehensibly any longer. So, I get her a box of Kleenex and a drink (she finished half a bottle—that's why I had to go out and get new supplies), she eventually shakes herself out of her misery, and cries, 'The children! The children! Those bastards, the man I loved for ten years with all my heart, aided and now replaced by the man I've married, have been helping to kill the children!' That's how she said it."

Roger and Sandra sit in silence for a good while. Then Roger asks, "What did she do with all this information? Did she tell Archie he was rumbled, for instance? Or inform anyone else? The police? I don't know."

"She said she didn't know what to do. For Herbie, it was too late, of course. And in Archie's case, she confessed she was far too much of a coward to confront him about his 'other life', as she put it. If she told anyone, she imagined he would be arrested and jailed and—perhaps the true reason for her lack of action, who knows?—that she would lose the house and become destitute. Whereas if she did nothing, no one would ever know, and she could go on enjoying the good life. She had done nothing bad, as she said several times, presumably to justify her silence."

"Well, well, well. But now she *has* told someone. Why do you think she picked you, or this moment, particularly when she knows what I do for a living?"

"Who can tell these things, darling? We can blabber on about guilt and bad consciences or the need people have to share their darkest secrets with someone or other, but who knows, really? Maybe she's already regretting that she blurted all this out to me and is right now throwing things into suitcases to flee the country."

"Only in books and films, my dear, does the story continue like that. But, anyhow, you haven't told me about the Facebook page. Did she tell you what all that's about?"

"Of course. It's perhaps even her saving grace—not that I will allow myself to judge her about the whole business. She said she knew she had to do *something* with the information she'd chanced upon, something short of telling anyone, that is. First of all, she looked up 'Ghouta', to refresh her memory of what had gone on there. She said that we all forget so very quickly these things, as atrocities in the world follow each other in such quick succession. She was certainly right there, wasn't she? And she soon came across all those sickening photographs and videos that followed the chemical attacks. Children, women, whole families, dead right there in their homes or workplaces, and others dying in front of our eyes, foaming at the mouth, in spasms of agony. She completely cracked up talking about it. And couldn't stop repeating, 'Herbie, Archie, they helped, they sold their souls to kill all these people. And all for money, just money.' Eventually, she said, and here she was a bit confusing and confused, she decided that she must 'bear witness'—that was the expression she used, even though it's difficult to see how her actions achieved that, exactly. So she scanned the photographs she had found on another day Archie was at work and left the safe open and then set up that web page using the Ghouta anagram."

"What were her intentions, though?" Roger asks.

"She couldn't really explain. I suppose she thought somehow that she had done her bit to uncover the truth and come what may. Perhaps she thought no one would ever see them, or see them for what they were. Perhaps, though Herbie had practically been a child murderer, she still loved him and wanted a trace to be left publicly through the publication of the photos. I think we'd have to question Eva Braun to really understand anything. But all things considered, it's quite amazing that your people found them, isn't it?"

"Indeed. Perhaps Bowdler isn't so outrageously wrong with his supposition that everyone has dirty secrets."

"Two unrelated war criminals in our own neighbourhood, though? What are the chances of that happening? You wouldn't believe it if you found that in a novel, I can tell you. Where are you on our Sok, by the way? Any closer to setting him up for the scaffold too?"

"I wanted to talk to you about that, darling," says Roger. "Bowdler has told me to call off the dogs. He won't fund any more of my 'wild speculation', as he calls it, because the readers of the 'Hack' basically don't care about a forty-year-old genocide on the other side of the world. He'd rather see a good investigation into the price of chickens and why they've suddenly gone up sixteen percent."

"He really said that? God, what an awful man."

"Yes, alas, he did. But here's my question: I need five thousand to prove or disprove this identity question and he won't give it to me. I wanted your blessing to spend that out of my own pocket, from the sale of my old house."

Sandra got up from the table and kissed him on the forehead. "Of course, my dear. Your money is my money now we're married and I'd love my money to be spent in this way. Now, I'm going to lie down and sober up. I love you."

"Thanks, sweetheart. Now I'm going to start drinking too and think what next to do about Archie."

"They say you punched a policeman."

"I most certainly did not."

"What happened, then? Why are you being held?"

"For questioning, apparently. They asked me if I was related to the famous 'Roger P. of the Hack'. Not only did I deny it, I said I'd never even heard of you."

"You didn't need to do that, Sandra. The police are our friends, you know."

"Yours, perhaps. Not especially mine."

"And the punch, darling?"

"A complete misunderstanding. I tried to fist-bump—that's the expression, isn't it?—this nice young man, as a sign of solidarity in our common struggle against repression and crime, that of the Chinese in this case, but he didn't grasp the significance of my gesture and took it on his chin."

Roger laughed. "He was an extremely short policeman, I assume? Anyhow, sweetheart, I'll get you out of there in a jiffy. I've made the call already."

"I don't want that, you know, Roger. How can we possibly ever talk about justice again if you can get me off the hook because of who you are and what your rag represents?"

"As you like, darling. I respect that. They'll let you go anyhow, I'm sure. They've got it in for the Chinese too right now, since that general punch-up with the goons from the consulate. It would look bad to prosecute anyone right now for protesting against those swine. That copper will just have to swallow his pride, I reckon."

And, indeed, Sandra does come home a few hours later, without charge, just a verbal warning not to hit public servants again. Roger has the good sense not to contradict her when she says that justice has taken its normal course and that she has been vindicated.

Later, at dinner, Roger asks, with genuine interest and no implied judgement at all, whether Sandra believes that her demonstrations and protests, today's or any other, have any meaningful effect on anyone or anything. His paper has always ignored them, for example, unless there are injuries or deaths or fighting. Most of the other media, too, for that matter.

"Happily, we're not doing it for you, darling, nor your readers."

"For who, then, if not our public opinion?"

"As you know, I am a great embarrassment to my father, who's had to disown me more than once, though he loves me beyond words, but it was actually him who told me why I must keep on doing what I do. His work as a senior diplomat has given him enormous insight into these questions, as you may imagine. He makes several good points. Aside from the personal need to speak up for human rights—that's not his own stock in trade, as you may imagine in his line of work—he says, to use his own words, that 'it helps keep the pot of revolt boiling.' "

"Which means?"

"All these writers and artists, political dissidents, rights lawyers, religious and ethnic minorities—journalists, also, of course—who are being repressed, jailed, tortured, in these countries against which we demonstrate, desperately need to know that their plight, their sacrifice, if you like, is heard about, recognized, by the world. They have no particular illusions that we shall change their regimes, but they do gain some consolation. My father has occasionally managed to bully, bribe or barge his way into prisons in some of the countries in which he has served, to talk to some of these people, and they give the impression that they would simply go mad from grief, loneliness even, if they weren't aware that there were people elsewhere on this earth who believed in them, believed that they were fighting for a just cause, for universal human values, and sympathized with them. They rarely get any solace in their own countries because no one is allowed to express any solidarity with them, of course, or will end up in prison too."

"And do they really hear about you?"

"You'd be awfully surprised. In our brave new world of electronic media, no regime anywhere can entirely suppress the free flow of information. Maybe only one protest, or article, or prize award in a hundred reaches the ears of some of these poor women and men. But if and when it does, the succour can be immense."

"Clearly that's important," says Roger.

"But it's far from all. My father told me also that even a letter of remonstrance written to an oppressive regime may plant at least a seed of doubt. He once met the Minister of Information of an African dictatorship who had seen *my* name among the signatories of a protest against the jailing of a poet. This chap, who my father says is a good man, whispered to him: 'Tell your daughter to keep on writing and signing these letters! Each time I receive one, I'm obliged to draft a briefing note for all the ministers in the government, any of whom might be asked to justify the jailing when questioned by foreigners.' So this Minister of Information investigates and lays out such cases in great detail for his colleagues and suggests a few weak and lying excuses for them to use if challenged. He told my father that some of them were totally unaware that this poet or that lawyer was in prison, on spurious charges at that, and that it rattled some of them or at least put the worm in the fruit, as it were. Who knows, in one out of fifty cases, something might then actually happen towards getting these people out."

"I can see that."

"Last, but not least, to take my own case today or on any other of my demonstration days, it rattles the Ambassador or Consul or whatever representation they have to see and hear a lot of screaming men and women outside their front door telling them that they are bastards, thieves, murderers, torturers, or whatever is the flavour of the day. They know that their paymasters in Beijing, or Havana, or Caracas, or Rangoon, or Pyongyang, or Minsk, or Moscow, or Tehran, or Damascus, or wherever, are going to hear about it and not like it at all, not like the videos on social media, wonder why they are paying the diplomats to enjoy the good life abroad when they can't even stop the peasants of these countries from making a song and dance about their activities and painting them as criminals. And this they do not like at all, you know. It never ceases to astonish me but beyond all other concerns they are all sensitive to their reputations! Pure vanity. No one at all wants to be pointed out as an ugly, cruel dictator, apparently. They'd all rather be photographed with their sexy wives on the cover of Vogue magazine or Paris Match."

"Well, you've convinced *me*, darling, at least."

"One more then. But it's so difficult to get these things into people's skulls. I hear all the time, 'But what good does it do?', 'What use are protests?', 'We can't change anything from outside', and so on and so on. I've become convinced of one thing, though: Of course revolutions, the overthrow of governments, come from the actions of the people of those countries, but I'm sure that their efforts will rarely be enough if there isn't similar great pressure from the international community, the like-minded citizens of our democracies, for instance."

"I've advanced half the money to get the rest of the story on Sok, by the way."

"Good for you!"

"Yes, it will take a week or two, but our man there promises a full report on this butcher Khieu and, as part of the deal, formal identification from his old acquaintances on the pictures we've sent him. I think the noose is definitely tightening around our neighbour's neck."

We bring down the chicken crooks

Let me tell you, distinguished reader, how this story of Sok and Archie ends—or rather how it in some senses begins …

Roger now has pretty much all the information he's going to get on these two dregs of humanity. The report from Phnom Penh leaves no trace of doubt. Sok is Khieu. After his short but blood-soaked career as a genocidal killer, Khieu became a successful businessman, doing a brisk trade in stealing land from the dead or dispersed owners, selling it, and making a huge fortune in the process.

Archie's case is about as sown up as it will ever be. The 'Hack's' intelligence and foreign affairs connections do not deny that they might know something, but imply that the nation's integrity is at stake if they as much as hint at or confirm what it might be. Ha! That's a good one, isn't it?

So, what do I do now, Roger asks me?

You have no other option than to lay it all out on Fred Bowdler's desk and see what comes of it, I tell him. And so he does.

"I have two scandals for you," says Roger by way of introduction as he sits in front of his boss's desk with two thickish files in his hands.

"Please use the incredible pith with which our good Lord God has endowed you, and give it to me in short, Roger. I've a very busy day ahead."

Roger places the two dossiers on Bowdler's untidy desk, which is already crammed full of files, letters, books, and various personal objects, including the replica of a guillotine and another of an electric chair.

The Chief Editor waves the files away. "What I don't need is more paper. Just give me the kernel of the stories."

Roger does his best, coldly, as I have advised, keeping his passion, his emotion, his indignation, his anger, under check. Pithy, said the chief. Make the murder of three million people and the gassing of children a bit pithy, won't you, my boy? He tells Bowdler that the 'Hack' has identified, caught if you will, two war criminals, one of them our very own, and has evidence to expose them both, just shortly before informing the police, of course. And then he tells their stories. Briefly, as ordered.

When he's finished, Bowdler says: "I thought I told you to abandon that Cambodian story, that I wouldn't have a penny more spent on it?"

"Yes. I spent my own money for the final stage of the investigation."

"Good God, you really *should* be working for the Grauniad, as I suggested. That's the kind of thing those suckers would do too. In any case, I need to think about both of these cases and talk to a few people. I'll get back to you."

And that is that for today. He must *talk to a few people*. We can only imagine what kind of people, can't we? Those to whom we are beholden; those we support; those with whom we have joined in the pact with the devil; those who might just one day crown Bowdler's head with a very nice garland of laurels, at a very nice reception, in the palace, perhaps?

Leaving the Chief Editor's office, clutching his files that Bowdler can't be bothered to read, Roger announces solemnly: "The price of chickens has fallen back to its usual level. That's good news, isn't it, chief?"

"You see?" says Bowdler. "The power of the 'Hack'? *That's* what we're here for, Roger. *That's* why our readers love us. If we hadn't campaigned against those chicken crooks and their outrageous price gouging cartel nothing would have restrained them. *This* is what a free press is all about, *this* is what the 'Hack' is about."

A secret toast to vengeance

Whether or not Fred Bowdler ever *talked to a few people* about the Archie and Sok scandals, we do not know and now probably never shall. Roger's suspicion is that he only claimed he had done so in order to fob off his best reporter. But whether he did or did not, the verdict was the same: The *superior interests* of the nation, confirmed at the *highest* levels, required that the 'Hack' drop both stories like proverbial hot potatoes.

When Roger learns, through a one-minute call from Bowdler (who could have said it to his face, since his office is a mere one hundred yards away), that this is the state of affairs, he stops everything he's doing and goes home without a word to anyone.

Sandra, coming home from the bookshop, finds the forlorn boy with his habitual whisky tumbler sitting in the dark behind closed curtains.

"What are you doing here, at this time? You quite spooked me. And the curtains? There's brilliant sunshine outside, you know."

Roger grunts. "It's all over. It's all off. I've been ordered to shut down the Archie Samuels and Khieu Sen cases. And to do something *important* with my time."

"Dear me," says Sandra.

"We did bust the chicken cartel, though," Roger mumbles. "You have to admit *that*."

Sandra smiles. "So, where do we go from here? Perhaps I could get some of the gang together and march on Archie and Sok's homes, demanding justice for their victims?"

In truth, Roger barely hears her. He's going over it all in his mind. He asks *me* what he should do now. I help him set out the options. Go to another, serious paper with the story? Inform the police—not that they would take it all anywhere? Whip up a campaign on social media for action to be taken —Roger is an expert at creating hysteria, of course? But who would care? The tiny minority who can be moved to give a damn were, rightly, currently engaged in the fight against the repression of Afghan women by the Taliban, or mobilising help for Ukraine to defend itself against the Russian barbarians. Cambodia and Syria were old stories and would pass under the radar of attention and opinion.

Sandra has got herself a drink too, now, as Roger finally speaks again.

"I could resign, of course, but no one would give a toss, really, and I wouldn't be better off trying to do something from the dole queue, anyhow. Yes, it would assuage my conscience for five minutes, but wouldn't advance anything. After all, I'm not being asked to do something that is against my principles; I'm being asked *not* to do something which is very much in their favour, that's all. I don't know, my love, I need to think this over, clearly. In the meantime, I've booked a restaurant for lunch. Would you like that? It's the one where we first properly met and talked and I made my first confession to you, that I worked on the 'Hack', you remember. I checked that they don't have any bloody chicken on the menu today, so we can think about something else, be romantic, perhaps? Would you like that, sweetheart?"

"I cannot think of anything in the world that I would like more right now than to return to the place where the love of my life introduced himself," Sandra replies.

And off they go. At the restaurant, the maître d'hôtel shows only by a faint flicker of a smile in his eyes that he recognizes Roger and his lady and leads them to a table, remarkably enough the *exact same table*.

"That's so sweet of you, darling, the same table!" exclaims Sandra.

Roger had not at all opted to ask for any particular table in his last-minute reservation. This guy must have been a casino physiognomist, he thinks. Anyhow, it's nice he believes I'm still into shady assignations, he tells me; I like that.

The love birds hold hands across the table and whisper sweet nothings to each other, remembering their foray into the 'Ws' and 'Bs' and much else of their early romancing.

Meanwhile, thanks to an odd but very useful brain evolution that nature has bestowed upon him and on many other men and women too, including you perhaps, dear reader—who knows?—he is at the same time having an intense and clandestine conversation with me about justice and how to achieve it in two particular cases that have come to obsess him.

You don't doubt that this is possible, do you? To have two entirely separate, simultaneous conversations going on like this? Well, it is so whether you doubt it or you don't. Roger discovered it for the first time a few years ago when he was giving a conference speech on some complicated matter or other and at the exact same time weighing up the chances of several horses who would run that afternoon in one of the biggest races of the year. No one noticed that they did not have his full and witty attention, no more than Sandra does now, because it isn't pretense of any kind and doesn't for a moment take away his feeling and sincerity about what he's saying to her. The human mind is a remarkable machine, isn't it? There are more things in a man's brain, my friends, than are dreamt of in your psychology. To whom it may concern.

Anyhow …

You know that there's no recourse through justice, don't you, Roger asks me? Not formal justice, in any case, not courts, nor enquiries, nor tribunals. Or there might be, in Khieu's case, after all, but it would take twenty years and then he'd be judged too old to stand trial if even he was still alive by that time. I don't know if the Cambodians would be interested now in the slightest, anyhow. He didn't become a successful businessman—*under his own name*!—without a great web of complicity. I guess that there were too many people in high places who benefited from his scams, shared his fortune. As for our own government, I'm absolutely positive that they couldn't be arsed to lift a finger. Apart from admitting that mistakes were made in the first place in allowing him to come here, they would have to spend an awful lot of money on bringing him to account, and they are far too busy stuffing all that's available into their own pockets and those of their friends. As for Archie, our arch poison killer, it's clear he's protected; he's a walking classified secret, that man. Draw the conclusions from that which you may.

I can't contradict any of this, Roger, I tell him. I'm afraid you are right. You often are, you know, when you talk from your reason and not your emotion.

Fine, fine, he chides me. What I do not need right now is one more of your moral lectures, Mister 2+2. I'm going to have to do justice myself, you know.

I feared that you were moving in that direction, toward that conclusion, I answer.

"Well, my darling" says Roger suddenly, raising his glass of champagne. "To us, to justice, to reason, to truth, to love."

"We have a lot of drinking to do today, that's clear," says Sandra tenderly, throwing a glassful brusquely down her throat. "Let's get started!"

I'm glad that the boy didn't toast also to quite another desire that had taken root in his mind: "To vengeance!"

Please do not jump from the cliffs

The choice of location for Roger P.'s murders came to him on an agreeable excursion with his wife to the seaside.

At breakfast today, Sandra suggests they both call in sick and leave the city and the human race behind them for a few hours. She knows an isolated cove on the coast where few go, and at this time of the year, mid-autumn, most likely no one at all.

"Fantastic idea," says Roger. "How about a picnic basket? Have we got enough in the house to throw one together? I'll organise the booze and some coffee."

"I'll rustle up something, for sure. Let's get going!"

Sandra's secluded cove is surprisingly near the city and they are there in little more than an hour and a half.

"My father used to bring me here," she tells Roger as they leave the main road and drive along a country lane toward the sea. "When we'd both had enough of mother, to tell the truth, and wanted a few hours alone. She never actually knew we came *here*. Father said that she would otherwise be jealous, probably angry, even though she would have refused to come along anyhow if he'd proposed it, such are irrational people, so we rather invented stupid missions like having to find a rare spare part for the car in another, distant town. She never asked questions about those kind of practical matters, because there was—is—little that interests her less."

"And you never felt bad about the deception, either of you?"

"I don't know about my father because he's never talked about his feelings. It's a mystery to me how he manages to keep everything within himself like that, but it seems to be a national characteristic, particularly in his own and previous generations. They are all complete strangers to each other, that's what they are."

"Yes, my parents are no different, nor their few friends. Some deeply puritan instinct of discretion or something still lives on within them all. Thank God we are different now, most of us, anyhow. I've always felt that if you don't express what you feel in one way or another it might as well just not exist at all. Walking shadows, those generations, that's what they are. What shall we ever remember of our mothers and fathers and their lives when they're gone?"

They have arrived as close as a car is able to go. Sandra indicates a narrow footpath through the long grass, practically hidden, and she leads him several hundred yards further until they come to a small opening from where they can see the sea glinting in the sunlight far below and before them.

"That's helpful," says Roger, laughing and pointing to a sign that confronts them. "*'Please Do Not Jump From The Cliffs'*," he reads out loud. "Good advice, I'd say," as he walks near to the edge and peers over. "Definitely not recommended for your health."

"Be careful, though, darling. It looks very dangerous over there anyhow. When I came with my father, I remember a fence all along that stretch, a good three or four yards before the drop. I don't know why it's not there any longer, frankly."

"Perhaps it dropped—or jumped—into the sea itself," says Roger. "These cliffs are eroding all along the coast, you know. Perhaps the chunk we're standing on will slide off as we picnic."

"That's not at all funny, my dear. But you come back here, please. Get us a drink—heavy on the tonic, for me, I'm driving home—while I prepare lunch." And with that she spreads a blanket over the ground, having stepped back a further fifty yards after Roger's bad joke, opens the picnic basket and organises their little feast.

Basking in the autumn sun, they talk about the future.

"I'll have to get out, you know," says Roger. "The fifth

column idea was a good one, but a one-man fifth column isn't going to achieve anything. I've been listening attentively to all my colleagues since I went underground for the enemy—that's you, basically, and the millions like you who've had enough. I haven't identified a single one of them who I think I could get to challenge 'The Hack's' *fundamental values,* if I can so dishonour the word by applying it to our motives. In the eight or nine years I've been at the paper, I haven't witnessed one single case where anyone questioned the morality, for want of a better word, of anything we did. Nor suggested that we should get interested in any issues purely on the grounds of their objective importance to society. We're bragging and boasting all the time about 'The Hack' being *the people's voice*; we even dare claim that we are *fearless,* for Christ's sake, in their defence—when the truth is we're cowards who would sell anyone at all down the river if it would please our bosses and help our circulation."

Sandra lets the boy talk; it's one of her many great qualities to listen well.

"No, I'll have to get out. I could get myself fired, of course, by slipping in a few honest stories about the government's grotesque lies on this or that subject when Bowdler has a day off, but that's not very honourable either."

"You could come and work in the bookshop, you know. I'll appoint you sales and marketing manager, if you like. I'll order a couple of hundred copies of Heinrich Böll and you can stand in the entrance trying to sell them. The enlightenment of the people about tabloid newspapers will be your first task in this new life."

They both smile wistfully. As things stand, they know they couldn't live long on the pittance the shop brings in. They both understand that without needing to say it to each other. They simply embrace in silence.

Roger now has two things to figure out: He needs a realistic plan to escape from the 'Hack'. And, more importantly, he must decide how best men's justice can be wrought upon two of his neighbours who have sinned far beyond any possible redemption. As they pack the picnic basket and gather up the blanket, he takes a last look at the shimmering sea and again sees the signpost, which seems to be calling to him, as though it were a personal message.

'Please Do Not Jump From The Cliffs.'

Dropping bombs

Should only the innocent be permitted to judge and punish others? Roger, my boy, that's your philosophical question of the day.

It's rarely if ever been that way, in any case, he tells me. It's even impossible, it seems, in the context of war. *Victors' justice* isn't an idle notion, at all. Imagine if Harry Truman had been on the wrong side? Killing two hundred thousand Japanese civilians with his A bombs. Result? Statues of him all over the United States. Whereas on the simple basis of his acts he should rather be a prominent chapter in the annals of war criminals, shouldn't he?

That's a reasonable proposition, I tell him, though you won't win any friends from it. Indeed, you could develop a pretty similar argument for Winston Churchill's guilt along those lines, if you felt like it. Many do. All those German cities pummelled to ruins, tens of thousands of civilians killed.

It's delicate to say it, though, isn't it, he remarks? It sounds like equivalence with the crimes of our enemies, though there is none; no one would understand it. We were the victors, yes, but we were the aggressed, the Americans too. And that's where most people choose to leave the question. Perhaps they are right to do so, after all. We can only try and be better people and better nations, right now and into the future.

Indeed, Roger. The important thing is surely to examine coldly what we've done anyhow without our vision being impaired by flags and anthems. Not a lot of people or nations have the taste and courage for that, it's true. Look how difficult even it's proving for you as an individual.

I know what you're implying, he tells me. You still want me to answer your question, don't you? Have I destroyed anyone's life? Do I have my own Katharina Blum? I think we have to tell the story and let us both judge.

A shabby little tale

A story within our story, then. You are lucky, dear reader. You were not promised two stories at all and I certainly didn't know at the outset that you would be getting this second one. I didn't know then that Roger would cough it up, to tell the truth, because the story doesn't shine particularly well on him and I'm certainly not writing this to aggravate his case. It's actually a rather unpleasant story and perhaps I should dispense with it rather rapidly.

As I wrote earlier while describing Roger P.'s first years at 'The Daily Hack', he was called upon to perform some rather disgraceful acts. I have mentioned that he bullied the relatives of the victims of the most abominable crimes and terrible accidents, their friends too, of course, into handing over photographs, but also various personal effects such as letters, diaries, even sometimes clothes similar to those worn by the victims at the time of the crimes to add a little colour to the illustrations of their deaths. Roger stole dead girls' dolls and once even a boy's pet cat, to take pictures of it and soften up the readers of his ghoulish stories. The cat escaped and was never heard of again. The 'Hack' told its readers that it had died from grief.

Aside from this contemptible looting of people's lives, emotions and memories, the 'Hack's' most prized stories, the ones that excite most its journalists, and doubtless its readers too, are to be found at the confluence of sex and politics. Happily for all concerned, the corridors of power continue to resemble those of a dimly lit bordello, as has always been the case, so there is much to investigate.

Roger chanced upon his greatest scoop in the matter in a rather roundabout way. A call girl had been stabbed to death and one of his team had acquired her diaries from the grasping concierge who discovered her body in his upmarket apartment suites. You never knew what might be found in such papers … Roger studied the diaries attentively and came across a reference that he suspected might lead to something. The murdered woman had written not only about herself, but about a few of her closest friends and colleagues. In one passage, she had recounted that one of them, outside the scope of her usual, paid work, had encountered a very senior member of the government and was drawing huge profit from their secret relationship. In short, he had set her up in regular business and directed certain public subsidies in her direction. The murdered girl wrote that she too hoped one day for such a fairy tale ending to a life selling her body.

The concierge had also sold Roger's reporter a small notebook with a few dozen telephone numbers—you never knew—and this friend was listed. Roger called her and asked to meet. She first refused, but after a few not very veiled threats of unspoken 'Hack' exposure, reluctantly agreed to do so.

Roger and D., as we shall call her, met at what became 'The Philistine'. The tavernkeeper gave them the semi-private alcove just off the main room, and there they discussed business. Roger told her of the very indiscreet diaries of her dead friend and how he knew about D.'s relationship and corrupt dealings with a government Minister. The 'Hack' was going to publish the story, of course, but if she would cooperate and tell it from her perspective, he could offer her a considerable sum of money.

The poor girl was absolutely distraught. She had left the call-girl profession behind her and rebuilt her life as a respectable woman. She had given no thought at all to the fact that her politician 'friend' had used public funds to help her. He had said something about it being a discreet government initiative to help unfortunate people like her to change their lives. Perhaps she had been naive, or had wilfully turned away from the obvious truth, but she was trying desperately to save herself and who could reproach her for that?

As she talked and talked, Roger was writing the story in his mind and, above all, the headline. What a tale! 'Minister Keeps Publicly-Funded Call Girl!' No … 'Minister In Private Sex Subsidy Scandal' …

D. begged Roger to keep her out of his story. It would destroy everything she had achieved in making a new life for herself; she would be thrown deeply in debt when the state asked for its money back; she had a child to feed and clothe. She would be ruined and publicly shamed too.

Had your fun, my boy, I asked Roger as he sat staring at the weeping woman? Got your scoop? And then he got up and left, leaving a few banknotes on the table and his telephone number.

Roger called the Minister early next day.

"You're finished," he told him coldly.

"I beg your pardon?"

"You're resigning from the government today."

"What on earth do you mean? Is this some kind of joke call?"

"No, either you resign by, let's say, mid-day, or early this afternoon 'The Daily Hack's' website, as a prelude to the full story in our print edition tomorrow, will announce that you have been keeping a mistress entirely funded by the public purse. I'm sure your wife will appreciate you didn't use the family budget."

There was a great silence on the line. Then, simply, "I see," then "Of course," followed by more silence and eventually nothing. The Minister had hung up. An hour later, the internet was submerged with stories about the sudden, unexplained resignation of the man destined, some said, to one day lead the country.

He was never heard of again. His political life, perhaps simply his life, was over, destroyed, and no one except Roger understood why.

D. called Roger a day or two later and simply said, "He told me you wouldn't run our story. Thanks. You're a good man."

As Roger recalls this distasteful little tale, he says to me: "It was your doing, of course. You stopped me from making a very big mistake. I'm grateful. Perhaps I did destroy this man's life, but I preserved hers. I hope that you will consider that we are quits now."

A good day for dying

Roger P. is going to kill Archie and Sok today. He hopes the two of them will go to hell on the same shuttle.

I invite Roger to consider whether it's wise to murder them both at the same time. (We are at present keeping his assassination plans on the level of banter. I don't think he will go through with them, to be honest. And I'll try and stop him if he's serious, that goes without saying. Right now, I cannot be certain whether I'll be able to or not, though, such is the man's hatred for his future victims and his despair that no one will allow for them to be held to account).

Did it ever occur to you that two men falling off a cliff is less suspicious than one, he asks me?

It may well be so, Roger, indeed.

But how did we get to this point anyhow, dear readers? I haven't told you yet, have I? For that, we must go a little back in time once more …

As men and women imbued with a compelling sense of justice, a love for right to triumph over wrong, as I do not doubt for an instant I can so characterise you, ladies and gentlemen, have you ever considered the greatest crime of our time and perhaps of any time, the genocide of the Jews, the Holocaust (not to overlook for one instant those countless others—Romas, Russians, Poles, homosexuals, the disabled, communists, socialists, Jehovah's Witnesses, others—who were also murdered, often in the same places with the same methods) and what became of the tens, let's rather say hundreds of thousands of Germans, perhaps as much as a million, if you think about it, who were either directly responsible or in some way complicit in these crimes? A few dozen trials, here and there? A modest number of executions, together with some extrajudicial killings? And then the imprisoned, all but a handful released after serving only a few years of their sentences? Have you ever wondered what you personally would have done if your parents, your spouse, your children, your whole extended family beyond that, had been coldly slaughtered in the Germans' camps or by their execution troops? And you had survived?

Roger has thought about these questions for a long time now. In fact, he began to do so well before two war criminals fell into his very own hands. He is bewildered that so many people, those closest to the victims, of course, but most importantly also the authorities of all the victor nations who had the requisite power, did so little to make the assassins pay the price, any price, for their killings and even let the overwhelming majority back into normal life, to take up the jobs and businesses they had been engaged in before the war, to raise families, perhaps, to spend time with their children. *To rebuild Germany* as a stable, democratic state, opposed to the new communist threat from the east, they argued in their defence when questions were raised many years later. Today still, of course, the timid national conscience of the Germans themselves continues to twitch a little as they finally pursue a handful of concentration camp guards and similar low ranking murderers, now geriatrics, seventy years after their crimes.

Thinking about all this, Roger has been doing his homework on vengeance and retribution. He finds isolated cases of war criminals tracked down and executed out of the public eye, and even an organized band of Jewish ex-partisans who planned and failed to commit a revenge genocide on millions of Germans by poisoning their water supplies. For the most part, though, the survivors set about reconstructing their own lives, for most of them far from the scenes of the atrocities that had wiped out their kinfolk. And absolutely no one has the right to judge them for that, in Roger's opinion, only to admire their breathtaking, almost incomprehensible fortitude.

Some of us may ask ourselves hypothetically how we would act in such extreme situations, which is really quite idle and gratuitous, because I doubt that we have any idea at all, and that *were* similar circumstances to arise for us we would most likely not behave as we thought we would. Nevertheless, Roger, who has no personal attachments to any of this, is so deeply disturbed by the immense, unspeakable injustice of allowing the murderers for the most part to go scot free, that he has often asked himself that precise question: What would I, as a survivor, have done, if ever I could have, as I saw our governments turn their backs on the victims? And he has always come to exactly the same conclusion: My sense of justice would force me to go on a killing spree against the perpetrators of the murders. An eye for an eye, or something like that (reading the bible is not high in his priorities for becoming an educated man and he hasn't got round to it yet and, I suspect, never will, however fine they claim it is). The idea that a man who has coldly killed others or enabled their deaths should be walking around free, as a car salesman or property agent, even perhaps in the very town where he has taken their lives, is so monstrous to Roger that he believes he would have no other option than to wipe these insults to humanity off the face of the earth.

Roger had, as I say, thought about all of this and formed his opinions well before Archie and Sok appeared in his life. Now he has the opportunity, or rather the obligation, as he sees it, to put his views into practice. He is no more personally implicated than he ever was for the victims of the Germans. But he persuades himself that in this matter of justice we are all responsible for each other. Who else will bring Sok, Khieu, to account now? Who will honour *his* victims? No one who can do something about it cares any longer, if they ever really did. And Archie? He is a classified secret, thanks to the authorities, and they are letting sleeping dogs lie …

I must kill them, Roger tells me. I have exhausted all other channels of bringing them to justice. Sok, whose dog plays with a human bone—perhaps a 'souvenir' of the killing fields? Who moves around the country, changing homes every year or two, lest exiled compatriots, perhaps, should finally catch up with him and do exactly what I have in mind myself. Can he really be allowed to live out his days here in peace? What a mockery to humanity that would be. And Archie? In a way, his case disgusts me even more profoundly than Sok, if that's possible. He has no blood directly on his hands; he had no personal knowledge of the victims. He's not an ordinary homicidal maniac, like Sok. He is no less responsible, though. He exchanged his expertise, as Baker did too, for death money. Perhaps his 'Ghouta bonus' was calculated on the number of people who were killed by his sarin? I'll have to ask him before he dies, won't I?

I let the boy rant to himself. At moments like this, in the hot rush of passion to his head, it's rather difficult to reason with him. The day will be long, though, and there will be other opportunities.

Roger has packed some good snacks, plenty of wine, coffee, and a pliable table and chairs from the garden. After picking up Sok, he drives the five minutes to Archie's home and, after introductions have been made, they set off toward the coast and a destiny of one kind or another for all of them. It had been easy to get them to come, though less so to overcome Sandra's reticence. I suppose she suspected he had something in mind other than "a fun afternoon out with my war criminals" during which he intended "to plunge the depths of the human soul, as part of my education," as he put it. But she didn't press him; she rarely if ever does. He will be sure to tell her all about it later.

"I'm so glad that I could get the three of us together like this," says Roger over his shoulder in the car. "I'm so busy at work these days and rarely if ever have any time to socialise. I'm glad too that you two could meet each other. You have a lot of things in common."

Neither of them question what such things might be. I suppose they think it would be churlish to express surprise at such an affirmation. Who knows? In any case, after a few banalities about how they like living in the village, both men fall silent, perhaps because they can think of nothing to say to one another. It's possible. They are not professional conversationalists like Roger, after all.

They go, of course, to Sandra's childhood cove.

'*Please Do Not Jump From The Cliffs.*' The signpost is still there, invitingly.

The men set up the table and chairs and Roger serves drinks and lays out the snacks.

"I hope that you like the view," says Roger. "It's magnificent, isn't it? A man could almost die happy if it were the last glimpse of earth he ever saw, don't you think?"

Sok and Archie smile and nod and Roger raises his glass and clinks it against both of theirs.

I ask Roger to explain his plan to me.

It's simple, he says. When we've had a few more (did you notice that they're both drinking a lot?) we shall go together and peer into the void, to see the beach below, and then we'll see if they can fly, won't we? That's after my interrogations, of course.

You're drinking a lot too, my boy, I tell him. Can you still think clearly?

My thinking has already been done, as you know.

One last try, though, to dissuade you, I beg him. Let's set out the facts. These men are war criminals, there is no doubt about that. They deserve to be tried and given appropriate punishment, yes. But, for reasons beyond our control, this is not going to happen.

So, I must take the matter into my own hands. You will tell me: What if everyone meted out his own justice and punishment? There would be a bloodbath in every street in the land. Many innocents would die, apart from anything else. That's your argument against my killing them, isn't it?

In short, yes.

And in long?

Well, for example, the death penalty has rightly been abolished in most of the civilised world, including here. Aren't you against it too?

The readers of the 'Hack' want it reintroduced, you know.

But you have become a civilised and modestly cultivated man, Roger. The 'Hack' readers are no longer your kind, no longer your gauge, either, for forming opinions. You're your own man now.

There's a difference, though, he tells me, between executing people for one or a handful of murders committed because of some dreadful deviancy or other, child killers, for instance (that's people's favourite example, of course), and the murder of hundreds or thousands of people for financial gain—Archie's case—or for supposed ideological causes, like those embraced by Sok. Who would claim it was wrong to hang the camp commander of Auschwitz, Rudolf Höss, for perfecting and implementing the vast murder machine that killed millions? Or, later, Adolf Eichmann, a key figure in the organisation of the Holocaust? Both of whom, not incidentally, I feel, died babbling about God. Do you, my spectator friend, feel bad about *their* executions? Would they not be right and appropriate today again? And the next time too that we have to try such men, as we shall, inevitably, because a crime like this on a mass scale is always just around the corner, of course. I must object also that capital punishment and the death penalty are affairs of the state and perhaps indeed a nation should not itself take lives, that's certainly open to debate. In the present case, though, I am simply a man, an individual, with a private duty to perform and if caught, which I don't intend to happen, will have to pay for his beliefs.

I'm happy that Roger has found his own voice, at least; at last, I could say too. It's a great tribute to his sense of survival and his need to put his past behind him. But what more can I say against his arguments? One more thing, perhaps.

Your form of personal justice is also never-ending, I tell him, you do realise that? By your logic, some individual could come after *you*, and then someone after him or her, and so on. With people as with nations, someone has to find it in themselves to break this chain of murder.

Let's see, says Roger, who has listened in good grace to my words. But now, to the immediate business in hand.

"Sok, Archie, I have a few things to tell you. Come and sit down."

The men, who have been loosening their legs a few yards away, do as asked.

"I've brought you out here for a reckoning. Yes, I suppose that's what this is about. I'm very interested about questions of remorse and regret and conscience and I want to examine your cases a little more closely."

Sok looks completely blank. Archie shifts in his chair and says, "Here we were, having a drink and making friends and admiring the beautiful sea view, and you want to interrogate us for a newspaper feature, I suppose. Are you creating a section on psychology, Roger? That doesn't sound very much like 'The Daily Hack'." He laughs.

"Well, it's not exactly that," Roger continues. "It's rather more a personal matter. My paper isn't interested in either of you, unfortunately. Gassing families in Syria, or smashing children's heads against trees in the killing fields of Cambodia, these aren't matters for our tabloid press, least of all the 'Hack', of course. We don't want to upset people, do we?"

"What he talk about?" Sok asks Archie, who shrugs.

"Sok," says Roger, "I propose that I call you Khieu, actually, Khieu Sen, isn't it?"

"What does he mean?" Archie asks Sok.

"How you know?" Sok asks Roger.

"It's a long story. But let me fill Archie in. Archie, little old Sok here is wanted in Cambodia for crimes against humanity. He has personally tortured and executed hundreds of men, women and children while supervising 'security' at a death camp. His real name is Khieu Sen and he's been on the run for almost twenty years. Hiding in the villages and towns of our little country, always on the move in case some of his compatriots, presumably, catch up with him."

"But," begins Archie.

"Don't worry, Archie, I'm coming to your case very soon. A little patience, please. So, Sok-Khieu, what do you have to say for yourself?"

"Terrible times," says Sok, staring into the void. "Must do these things. Orders. Or me killed too. And family."

"Nothing new under the sun, then, Khieu. Just following orders, afraid for your own life. I don't believe a word of it, unfortunately for you. I've read some of the statements from the very few survivors of your camp. You were a brute, an animal, of the most vicious kind, and took great pleasure, far beyond what anyone would have demanded of you, in your sadistic work. This is the truth."

Sok says nothing at all. Doesn't weep, nor look anguished, nor defend himself, nor protest. Nothing. Just continues to stare into space. He's perhaps emptied his mind completely, thinks Roger.

At this moment, Archie has apparently had enough and gets up to leave.

"Sit down, Archie. Let's get straight to the point: How much was your share of the Ghouta bonus? How much does Syria pay for your sarin expertise? Enough to buy that fancy house of yours, I imagine."

"Now hang on," begins Archie. "I've no idea what on earth you're implying."

"I'm not *implying* anything," says Roger. "I'm telling you straight out. Not only do I know about your traffic in biological weapons, but I have the proof. You're a cold-blooded murderer, just like Sok here. Once or twice removed, of course. But that doesn't make you any less guilty. I have all the evidence I need to expose your dirty little racket of supplying the expertise, perhaps even the goods themselves."

"Evidence? There's no evidence," says Archie, who appears already to have dropped his denial that he has any knowledge of what Roger is talking about. "You're making it up. What do you think you know about any of all this?"

"Sheila has spilled the beans, Archie. That's the thing about betrayal; you never know who's going to be next in line. It's your turn."

"Sheila?" he laughs. "She knows nothing at all. I never told her anything."

"Perhaps she got hold of Herbie's papers? Did you ever think of that? You really should lock your safe, you know. And while you're at it be more attentive to what your wife publishes on Facebook. It's all there, the photos too. The ones you stole from Baker's study."

Archie looks completely stunned about what he is hearing and falls silent. Sok has crumpled up on his chair, his head between his knees. Roger clearly isn't going to learn anything more from either of them. And in truth, he has lost his taste for the whole business.

"It's the end of the road, guys," says Roger. "Have a few more drinks. I'll leave the bottles, even the corkscrew. Ignore the sign. Please *do* jump from the cliffs."

And with that, he turns and walks back through the thick undergrowth towards the car, shouting over his shoulder, "You'll have to find your own way home, I'm afraid. Hitch a ride, perhaps. See you both in the war crimes tribunal, after we've published your stories in the 'Hack', of course."

Roger takes nothing with him. He has never liked the table and chairs set, anyhow.

"It's almost dark, we'll never find our way out of here," Archie calls after him.

"Now what a shame that would be," are Roger's last words.

You did the right thing to do nothing, I tell Roger as he heads for home.

I know, he replies. And do you know how I know? Not because of any particular argument for or against killing these scum. But because I suddenly feel complete personal indifference to their fate and that is so much more powerful than any pleasure I might have gained from pushing them over the cliff. That's strange, isn't it? For weeks now I have hated these men deeply and looked forward to killing them. And now I couldn't give a damn what happens to them. How strange is the human mind. At least they will now live in fear that their sordid, abject lives are going to be exposed, or at least that they think it's so. They'll have to live knowing that they are hunted men. But is it really possible that indifference can be stronger than vengeance, he asks me? Surely not?

If that's what you feel, I tell him. It will certainly help you suffer less. Others may feel differently. And all feelings, as you know ...

... are authentic, he interrupts me. Yes, I haven't forgotten your belief about that, he says. How could I, since you're always on about it?

We laugh.

"So, there you are!" Sandra greets Roger at their house door. "Sheila has called twice to ask when Archie will be home; his mobile doesn't work."

"It could be a rather long wait, I think. I left them to walk back."

"You didn't? What a very naughty boy you are, my husband!"

"Yes. I also had it out with them. Told them we knew everything about their vile pasts and their dreadful crimes."

"Good Lord. How did they react?"

"Sok didn't even deny that he was Khieu Sen. He just mumbled a pitiful handful of words right out of the political and military murderer's handbook. I was only following orders. If it hadn't been them, it would have been me. Nothing new under the sun. Then he seemed to completely collapse from within and I left him in a heap on the table."

"And Archie?"

"Archie's made of tougher stuff, for sure. He *did* try to claim he didn't know what I was talking about and said I couldn't possibly have any evidence to back my assertions. Then I told him about the papers and the photos on Facebook and Sheila's confession."

"Did you have to drag her into this? I feel bad about that. That she knows I repeated everything she said to you."

"At that particular moment, it wouldn't have mattered, darling. Because I had intended to kill them both."

"Good Lord. That would have been a fine mess."

"I planned to do it so it looked like an accident, of course. But it didn't happen, in any case, so it's useless to go over it."

"What do you think you've achieved, then, if anything?"

"They must now feel hunted, tracked. I told them, I lied, that the 'Hack' was going to run their stories, expose them. I reckon that must have sent the fear of God through them."

"Maybe they'll run away."

"It's possible, of course. But that wouldn't be a bad punishment either, would it darling? That they should have to abandon everything and disappear into clandestine lives, afraid at every moment of the tap on the door. I could hardly hope for more, could I, since justice *has* abandoned me?"

"You did well, my love, I can see that. They won't be sleeping easy any time soon, either of them. I guess, as a bonus, that old Archie will be thinking of Herbie Baker's mysterious death, too, and wondering whether a similar fate is awaiting him one day when the story's out. I think I'll take the telephone off the hook tonight, so Sheila can also begin to sweat it out for a while."

"Thanks for your understanding about all this, darling. I feel so much better now. That somehow justice has been served, however imperfectly. I also achieved one other important thing today."

"What was that?"

"I got rid of that bloody awful garden furniture your mother gave us. Just left it there."

"I never liked it either," Sandra confesses, laughing.

A visit from the police

Marjorie was the first to call him the next day. "Is that my investigation off, then, boss? Or what?"

"What do you mean?" asks Roger.

"Now Khieu is dead; you did hear about it?"

"No, I didn't hear anything at all. What are you talking about?"

"Those two bodies found on the beach early this morning. We had a couple of paragraphs in the last web update. They've already been identified. One of them was Sok, i.e. Khieu. He had his papers with him. They both did. The other chap was a certain Archie Samuels, a biochemist. Charlie tells me that you knew him too. That's odd, isn't it?"

Roger is stunned. "Who found them?"

"A crab fisher, apparently. They were in a right state, though. Badly smashed up. Looks like they fell off the cliffs."

"Look, Marjorie. Don't tell anyone about the link with our investigations for the moment. Make sure Charlie doesn't, either. And get me the name and number of the police chief dealing with the case."

Roger hangs up. And sits staring into himself. How the hell did that happen, he asks? Surely they didn't jump off the cliffs? That would be fairy tale stuff. I know it was getting dark; could they have had another drink or two in the dark and then walked in the wrong direction and fallen? Divine providence, or something?

I don't know, Roger, I tell him. But you'd better start talking very soon. You must let the police know you took them there, then abandoned them, even if it doesn't look very good, I admit. Sheila is probably blabbing already. They'll probably even call *you*.

And indeed, that's exactly what the police did. They said they would come up to town that very evening to talk things over with him. Roger arranged for them to meet at his club; they would like that.

Later, over drinks with the two detectives they had dispatched to "have a conversation" with him, as they put it, Roger told the story exactly how it happened, and how I have recounted it to you, dear reader. Except, wisely or unwisely (you can judge for yourself from subsequent developments), he chose not to mention his original objective for this excursion with his neighbours: he did not say that his intention had actually been to kill them. Detectives being detectives, that would most probably have aroused their suspicions … And since they were, in Roger's view, not the two sharpest pencils in the constabulary's drawers, they might not have easily entertained the idea that though this was his original purpose, he had abandoned the plan. 2+2 functions also in the minds of our police force sleuths, of course. Indeed, if it didn't, they could hardly do their jobs, could they?

All that Roger said that evening was diligently confined to notebooks. The police had said only that the investigation was 'ongoing' and that it would include a visit by a local geologist to determine whether there had been any recent movement in the land above the beach, where chunks of cliff were known to break off from time to time.

Roger and I had not thought of this possibility. So bravo to our fine policemen!

The tabloids have a field day

They came for Roger at dawn.

He would obligingly have responded voluntarily to any summons, but instead the police thought it useful to employ a large team of armed goons to break down both his front and back doors and scare the living daylights out of Sandra and Roger both.

The greatest quality of the police has never been to make subtle distinctions in such matters between casual suspects and hardened criminals known to shoot first. Perhaps they have superior and very fine ideas about equality before the law, who knows? Or perhaps they remembered Roger's recent 'Hack' articles accusing them of 'going soft' on crime in the capital?

The raid came three days after the pleasant conversation between Roger and the detectives at his club. What had happened in the intervening period? We didn't hear the full story until months later at his trial. In the meantime, held in detention while the nation's newspapers went wild with speculation at the rare event of a journalist being accused of murder, sweeping aside all the sub judice laws of the land in the process, the unlikely double killer tried to come to grips with his situation.

I don't stand a chance, Roger tells me one day, after speaking with one of his crime reporter colleagues from the 'Hack', who very kindly pays him a prison visit (subsequently turned into an enticing story for the paper, of course). They've got everything. Malice aforethought, as we used to say so prettily; now *mens rea*—intent to kill, if I've understood correctly. A motive. That could easily be construed from everything I've said to one person or another. The means—I didn't take them to the funfair, after all, but to the edge of a precipice.

All that's missing is any evidence, I tell him. Did you mention to anyone that you intended to kill them? No. Or rather only Sandra, after you came home, but she won't talk, of course. Surely it won't be enough that you only wanted to bring them—legally—to account? Though we have to say that it really doesn't look good, all of this, I admit.

I'm beginning to think it's easier to defend yourself against something you did than something you didn't do, Roger tells me despondently.

Isn't it about time you got a legal team, though? Perhaps there are things that we have overlooked.

No, says Roger, I'm going to defend myself, as I've always done inside or outside the courtroom. I don't want some complete stranger standing up and talking on my behalf. Either I convince the jury I'm innocent or I don't, but no one can do that for me.

Days go by like this. When he isn't thinking about his case, Roger spends his time reading. Sandra brings him the books he wants. He finds that one writer leads naturally to another, an uncanny affiliation in thoughts and ideas and perspectives on life. Sandra looks more destroyed and distraught at each visit and he fears seeing her again each time now. It's impossible to have more support and love than she gives him, but this does little to diminish his despair to find himself in prison. It even compounds it in many ways, since he has to see her suffer too. I'm sure she knows this and that she does her brave best to appear composed.

A date has been fixed for the trial. Roger has long ago been before the magistrates, where sending him to the higher court proves nothing but a formality, in view of the compelling case that the prosecutors have put together against him and the absence of any convincing defence except his innocence.

A psychologist flounders

Roger is obliged to go and see a psychiatrist before his case is heard. The meeting doesn't go well, all things considered.

"What do *you* do, then?" Roger asks, as they sit down in the man's office, a short drive from the prison.

"Didn't they tell you?"

"They said something about examining my mental state. I'm fine, though."

"I'm a criminal psychologist."

"Not a psychiatrist?"

"I'm both, actually."

"That's handy."

"Indeed. But we're here to talk about you, not me, of course."

"Sure. Though I imagine that *your* mental state is more interesting than mine, actually."

Don't be cheeky, Roger, I advise him.

Do you think I should play along, then, he asks me? I could also tell him to get stuffed, you know.

I'm not certain that your situation would be improved if you did, though I know it would be a pleasure for you.

You're right, he tells me, on both counts.

"Fine," Roger tells the psychologist. "How can I help you?"

"Tell me something about yourself, your childhood, your job."

"Not much to tell, really. I had a perfectly ordinary childhood. No one took any particular interest in me, and I didn't take much in them either, to be honest. I came to no harm."

"You feel that you were neglected?"

"No. Just an ordinary childhood of our times. I just went about my business as did everyone else. I got through school and then out of it at the first available opportunity."

"Why was that?"

"No special reason. It bored me to tears, that's all. I wanted to get out and discover the world rather than sitting in classrooms staring out the window. This so-called education wasn't doing me any good at all. I came out of school knowing precisely nothing about anything. Perhaps I wasn't paying sufficient attention, who knows? I don't blame anyone."

Roger pauses for more questions but none come. He thinks that either the psychologist isn't so curious about him after all, or that it's that timeworn technique where they just want you to go on blabbing about yourself in the hope that something meaningful finally emerges that they can get their fangs into.

Assuming it's the latter case, Roger drones on, about the newspaper and what he has done there over the past few years. Just the facts; nothing about what he feels about anything.

"Tell me about your relationship with these men you killed," the psychologist finally asks him.

"I didn't kill them, you git," Roger replies rudely. "Haven't you read the file? I am innocent of the charges against me."

"Let's not get insulting. I meant to say these men *you are accused of killing*, of course. I'm on your side, you know."

"No, I didn't know. How do you figure that one?"

"Are you impulsive and disinhibited, sometimes?"

"Look, Doc," says Roger. "Let's not play games. I didn't even enjoy them when I was a child. Just ask me specific, direct questions on the facts, and I can get out of here."

Do you think I should tell him about *you*, Roger asks me? That would set the cat among the pigeons, wouldn't it? He'll be taking me for Ted Bundy in no time.

I advise him against it. Very prejudicial. If the man learns that Roger has another voice in his mind, that'll open the floodgates to every flavour of insanity ever dreamt of in the history of criminal psychology. Maybe he wouldn't go to prison for life, but he'd be interned for ever in one of their hospitals, for sure.

"Would you like a coffee?"

"Yes, I would. Thanks."

The psychologist goes off, asking the police guard outside the door if he'd like a coffee too. Roger meanwhile stares out of the office window.

I could make a run for it right now, did you notice, Roger asks me? Like Ted Bundy, actually. He escaped from custody, believe it or not. Twice, in fact. But he didn't have any plans on the outside, except more crime. If one were to do it, one would have to be prepared in advance ... He is suddenly feeling more cooperative and thinking that perhaps coming here was not such a bad thing, after all.

"You were asking if I am impulsive," Roger tells the psychologist when he returns with the coffee. "I suppose I am, indeed. I like making decisions on the spur of the moment."

"Without much thought, then? Not reasoned?"

"No, I wouldn't say that. Don't you think that in most situations we find that we've already a history of reasoning and a pattern of behaviour? We don't start that all over again each time, do we? I think, nevertheless, that we still have choices: do it, don't do it, that kind of thing, and can decide in a flash. That's what I meant. It doesn't imply that we make mistakes, for all that. Just that there are constantly alternatives, several options even, at our disposal about what action to take. As for 'disinhibition'—I believe that's the word you used—I reckon I have the inhibitions of any normal person in society. I've never remarked the contrary, in any case."

That's it, my boy, I tell Roger. Talk the man into a stupor! Once you've got through with him, he'll wish he'd never taken on your case!

Roger is encouraged by my support and talks his head off for another half an hour on a dozen subjects that pass through his mind, all unrelated, happily, to war criminals, vengeance and justice. Maybe he will have to explain his views on all those questions in court, we haven't yet figured that one out. After all, with the evidence now available about his investigations into Sok and Archie, how could he possibly justify, other than with the dangerous truth, why he had taken them out to the seaside on an excursion in the first place? A real dilemma lies ahead, for sure.

In the meantime, I can't resist telling you already the conclusions of the psychologist's report read at his trial. Roger is "impulsive and narcissistic" and suffers at the same time from "obsessive compulsive and attention deficit hyperactivity disorders." And much else from the manuals of psychiatry. He is judged sane, though. For better or worse.

A truly shocking experiment

From the day of his arrest to the beginning of his trial, Roger P. spends six months in prison, which is quite a short wait as such things go in our times. For an innocent man, it is nevertheless an eternity, as you may imagine.

Roger has been placed in solitary confinement; he has a cell all to himself, in other words. This is not a punishment, though, as is usually the case. He is alone for his own protection. The prison authorities have judged that the 'Hack' has so many enemies that it wouldn't be impossible to find a few in this very prison who might want something unpleasant to happen to him.

We are delighted, Roger and me, with this situation, of course. We amuse and entertain ourselves very adequately alone. It has always been surprising for men who like to be alone, who perhaps even yearn for it, to hear that prisoners who are isolated in this way very often go crazy, or at least suffer terribly. They need, indiscriminately, the company of other men, it seems.

Though this has been known for centuries by torturers and punishers of all kinds, it was happily confirmed in recent years by another very amusing psychological research project undertaken by our dear American friends. Roger and I had a great laugh when we learnt about it, I can tell you.

A US university recruited hundreds of undergraduates and innocent civilians to undergo experiments of being shut alone in rooms with no means of communication or stimulation other than their own minds and thoughts. At one point, they are each confined in this way for fifteen minutes, equipped only with a button which they are told will give them a strong electric shock if they choose to press it. The poor, innocent psychology professors imagined that "it wouldn't be that hard for people to entertain themselves" alone for this short moment without self-inflicting physical pain. However … more than two-thirds of the men cracked before the quarter hour was up and actually electrocuted themselves! The brilliant conclusion of this and other experiments in the project was that men are "markedly less happy when spending time inside their heads."

That's amazing, don't you think? But one other thing: a little mystery of the electric shock business was that only twenty-five percent of the confined women, i.e. far, far fewer, pressed the button. Make of that what you will! It would clearly be a research project all of its own that would, though I reckon no one will dare to try and get to the bottom of the matter, since they might have to walk over very thin ice … (When Roger excitedly told Sandra the story on one of her visits, she said, as though it were the most obvious thing in the world: "Women aren't as stupid as men, that's not a scoop, darling. Deliberately electrocuting yourself, indeed.")

So, man is terrified of being left alone with himself to think! Think about that if you would. Or just ask Roger. Before he reached an accommodation with me, he might well have been one of these self-electrocutioners, we have to admit it, if he were deprived for fifteen minutes of his chosen *maelstrom of pleasure*, as we once so prettily described it.

To be honest with you, though, it would have been quite possible also for the psychologists in this lovely little experiment to have drawn a diametrically opposite conclusion than the one they came up with. That, paradoxically, those who pressed the button simply had much more going on up in their craniums than the others in the way of thought and that, far from the professors' expected *entertainment*, this was actually torturing them. I'm sure that you, like Roger, have from time to time had to wait not for fifteen minutes, but for an hour, two hours perhaps, in a hospital waiting room, and observed that the majority of people are quite capable of staring at the wall without even twitching all that time, their thinking processes apparently having not even been activated, and that you can spot the ones who clearly have something going on upstairs by their visible impatience, even distress. In other words, that it was not, as the psychologists supposed, that the electrocutioners were especially bored, but that they couldn't *handle* the thoughts they had to deal with. If we believe rather in this explanation, it's actually quite encouraging. It would mean that something was indeed going on in the heads of two-thirds of the men, but that they didn't like it at all. Couldn't control it, perhaps? Didn't, just for instance, have the quality of dialogue with themselves that Roger and I have established.

Who knows?

At first, Roger imagined that he would spend his pre-trial months studying homicide law in his cell, like they do in the movies, at least when the murderers have chosen to defend themselves. He acquired a handful of basic texts on the matter, but soon abandoned them. They were astonishingly tedious; we agreed on that. And had clearly not been written to help innocent men, either.

Roger thinks that his case is hopeless. Yes, the evidence against him is purely circumstantial, but everything points towards his guilt. At times, until I rein him in, he even develops the very arguments for his culpability. I wanted them dead, he tells me; I took them there with the intention of killing them; I abandoned them at nightfall in a dangerous spot. What more could you ask for as reasons for conviction? Only that you are nevertheless innocent, I remind him. And that no one at all, other than Sandra, of course, knows that you ever had plans for murder.

What do you think actually happened, he kept asking me? Do you think that they jumped, in some kind of desperate suicide pact, believing that their crimes were to be imminently exposed, and that they would be arrested and shamed and punished? Or did they simply fall in the dark; an act of providence? The geologist ruled out a landslide, unfortunately.

I could never give Roger a satisfactory answer, because there was no way anyone could ever know, of course. I like to think that they disobeyed the signpost and leapt to their deaths, knowing they were at the end of the road with no chance of escaping their fate. The only thing I'm sure we can rule out with certainty is that they killed themselves from guilt or remorse; that goes without saying.

This is not Kafka

What can I tell you about the trial, dear reader?

It was fair, at least, something for which we should all be grateful. In half the world today, verdicts are decided in advance and the judges do what they are told. The accused have little if any opportunity to defend themselves; they are often deprived of lawyers; the proceedings take place well away from the inquisitive eyes of the public and the press; there are no juries of the people. Yes, that is still the sad state of justice among men on much of our earth, I'm afraid. Even

Socrates got a better deal two thousand four hundred years ago.

Roger is allowed to talk himself to death if he wants. He has rejected legal representation, as I mentioned, but that's entirely his choice. No one can claim the judge has been told how to do his job; the relations between the judiciary and the government are sufficiently strained as it is without politicians daring to meddle in the cases of individuals.

The jury has been selected according to time-old practices and it wouldn't cross anyone's mind to suggest that they have been interfered with outside the courtroom. Yes, they bring with them each day, in addition to their sandwiches, a whole array of prejudices and surely also a rich variety of the famous *cognitive biases*, but there's not a lot anyone can do about that, is there? We don't know if they are readers of 'The Daily Hack', but it wouldn't be very surprising if at least some of them were. Whether this is helpful to Roger or unhelpful, it's impossible to say.

What is certain is that Roger quickly puts the judge in a bad mood when he is asked to confirm his name and his employment.

"Roger P., Your Worship. Investigations Editor at 'The Daily Hack'."

"Your Honour," says the judge.

"That's too much. Please do call me Roger."

The judge is not amused at all. Roger, please, behave yourself, I exhort him. This is not the time nor place for being a smartarse. The rest of your life is at stake!

"Let me tell you one thing before this trial gets underway, Roger P.," says the judge. "We are inclined to make certain allowances in cases where the defendants have chosen, wisely or not, to represent themselves. I'd like to make it clear that these do not extend to sarcasm or attempts at wit. The Court, Mr P., does not have a sense of humour, most particularly when the charge is one of murder, two murders, in your case."

In order to spare you a lot of tedious procedural matters and excruciating clarifications about this or that legal detail, dear, impatient reader, I shall condense this account of the trial itself in the same way as they do in the cinema.

The prosecution presents its case: Roger P. spent weeks investigating the pasts of his two victims and found that, *in his opinion*, they were both guilty of war crimes. Neither Sok Charya nor Archie Samuels are on trial, so the Court and the jury will not be asked whether or not there is any foundation at all to his accusations. That is in any case completely irrelevant, says the prosecutor, and can play no part in considerations of whether the defendant is guilty or innocent of murder as charged.

In short, Roger P., who was angry at what he suspected were their crimes, and deeply frustrated that they would never in his view be brought to justice, lured them out to a location which in everyone's estimation is extremely dangerous and, quite clearly, pushed them over the cliffs to resolve this internal conflict of his. The case is really cut and dried.

In support of this narrative, and aside from showing photographs of the cliffs, the picnic area, the beach and the broken bodies, the prosecution calls and examines only two essential witnesses—Sheila Samuels and Fred Bowdler, though various others briefly appear to confirm material aspects of the case. Roger will save his testimony by calling himself as a witness.

Sheila Samuels spends her time in the stand bawling her eyes out and adds little or nothing to the prosecution's case except, perhaps, to soften up the jurors. She confirms that the accused's wife has, in a most underhand manner, sought information of a slanderous nature about her ex-husband's professional activities, and passed it on to the defendant. All of which the court is now aware of from the prosecution's introductory remarks. She will say no more; may her Archie rest in peace.

For better or worse, Roger doesn't even bother to cross-examine her. We both agree that it would not produce any useful information and that he might worsen his standing in the eyes of the jury by appearing to bully the poor widow.

Fred Bowdler is another type of fish entirely. Roger and I have speculated in advance about his testimony, but have not been sure at all which way he might play it. He possesses most of the information to condemn Roger, but surely will be loyal to his favourite reporter and, without saying anything false, of course, will try and smooth things out for him.

We are rapidly proven comprehensively wrong.

As Bowdler takes the stand in turn, the judge asks him for a clarification on his identity.

"Was it not *your* newspaper, 'The Daily Hack', which infamously defamed several of my greatly esteemed colleagues with a front-page headline calling them 'Enemies of the People'?"

"No, no, Your Honour. That was another publication. We would never be so disrespectful."

The judge clears his throat, apparently to indicate his scepticism, and then signals to the prosecutor to get on with his witness examination.

Roger has thought to intervene and ask Bowdler if it is nevertheless true that they had investigated the judges in question, making homophobic remarks about one of them and implying that they were all three actually drunkards. I tell Roger sharply to keep quiet; we want Bowdler to be on our side, as far as it's possible.

Our hope is in vain.

Bowdler tells the Court that Roger P. was once his most prized reporter, but that he had gone completely downhill after becoming paranoiac about two of his friends and neighbours, who he set out, for reasons beyond Bowdler's comprehension, to cast as very wicked men, even war criminals, as the prosecution has said. Bowdler had thought from the very start that they were cock and bull stories, these allegations about Archie Samuels and biological weapons and this case of mistaken identity over an upstanding Cambodian refugee given shelter by our country. He had told Roger to cease his wild speculations and get back to his job of dealing with matters of immediate concern, in the current climate of crisis, about events in *this* country.

"What was Roger P.'s reaction to your refusal to let him pursue these fantasies?" asks the prosecutor.

"He got very angry. Spoke to me in a very insolent manner and told me he wouldn't leave things there, that he'd find a way of bringing these men to justice without the 'Hack's' help."

That was the case. In a nutshell. It doesn't matter in the slightest, Roger sees, that his so-called 'fantasies' are factually true. All the jury will need to understand is that he believed them to be true and that, as the judge explained to them at the outset, he thus had *reason and intent* to do these men harm, to exact his own justice.

Roger has only one question for Fred Bowdler in cross-examination.

"Isn't it true that when ordering me to cease my investigations into these cases, you actually told me: 'I'm not interested in your fucking war criminals or the fucking Cambodian genocide or fucking Syrian chemical attacks and nor are our fucking readers. I'm interested in the price of chickens.'? Or words to that effect. I just want the Court and the public to know what kind of a man and what kind of newspaper we're dealing with here."

Bowdler refuses even to answer the question and neither the prosecution nor judge insist that he should do so.

Where does all that leave us, Roger asks me during a recess before he presents his defence?

You have two options as I see it, I tell him. Say that you took Archie and Sok out on that trip in complete innocence, because you had forgiven them their crimes or just wanted to talk these matters over with them in the hope of persuading them to admit and accept what they had done and thus save their souls, or somesuch tripe. Say that you wouldn't have left your garden furniture at the scene as evidence if you had killed them, for example, or a few similar assertions to create doubt and confuse the jury. *Or* ... you could come clean, tell the truth from beginning to end and take your chances. You took them out there to the cove to kill them, it's true. You were going to push them over the cliffs while you were all looking down at the beach. But you *talked yourself out of it*. You decided that it was not for you to take justice into your own hands, however much they deserved to die, because if all men were to do thus, the world would be even more of a never-ending bloodbath than it is already.

And you, should I mention *you*? Socrates used his internal oracle as a defence, after all. He said that it would have prevented him from committing any crime.

Look where that got him, I say. I would, though, talk a little more about how a man can advise himself on the basis of reason that the actions he is intending to take are counter to the interests of the cause that he is pursuing, in our case seeking that justice should be done.

Do you think I have any chance with this approach?

No, not really. But since you are most likely going to be condemned either way, you could at least have the satisfaction that you chose the noble path of truth. That would be an excellent final act for you, wouldn't it? That's perhaps what we've been working on these past ten years, isn't it Roger? That you should embrace with courage your hard-won convictions and your love for reason and for the truth right at the precise moment when doing so might well actually worsen or even seal your fate.

You're right, Roger eventually concedes. Why lie and be condemned when I can tell the truth and be condemned? And so he does.

Roger explains, trying to respect the trial format with questions and answers to himself, that he was indeed outraged that Archie and Sok were leading comfortable, contented lives, even as the victims of their monstrous crimes were becoming a distant memory to our consciences, and that hardly anyone cared about that, least of all his own newspaper, for all its claim of being supposedly the people's voice. Having found no way else to ensure that they would ever be brought to account or ever stand trial, he had decided to do justice himself on behalf of the honour of men. He had taken them out to the cove on the coast with the intention of confronting them with their crimes, hearing any defence they might offer, while remaining willing to accept any claim to innocence they might make—neither of them even tried to exculpate themselves, he tells the Court—then to dispatch them over the cliffs on the way to whatever might or might not be awaiting them in the afterlife.

"However, I changed my mind, I did not lead them to the edge of the precipice, did not push them over, did not kill them," he continues, looking towards the men and women in the jury. "This is not so unusual, is it? We constantly plan actions that we then abandon, don't we? We are led by our emotions and instincts, our desires, our loves and our hatreds, our need for vengeance, perhaps, but we each have also within us the voice of truth and reason if only we will listen to it. Well, my voice called on me that day—we have a very vibrant relationship; he is there for me at all times—and told me that what I intended to do was wrong. That to kill these swine might perhaps serve the ideal of justice that collectively we were incapable of realising in their cases. But that one man, an individual, or even groups of men, come to that, could not take it upon themselves to decide for society to deprive other men of their lives. That such actions outside the framework of policing and laws and courts such as this one can under no circumstances be permitted because they can only lead to unceasing bloodshed and, inevitably, injustices and mistakes too. My inner voice told me this and I listened and I could not find an argument against him and as I was giving him his hearing I began to entirely lose my personal interest in seeing these men die. Strangely, I became indifferent to their fate; I had expended all my passion to see them punished. So, I left them both there with a couple of bottles of wine—the police have testified that they found five empty bottles in all—at dusk, turned my back on them and went home. I told them in parting that both their stories would feature prominently in coming editions of 'The Daily Hack'. Which, of course, had the tabloid press and its Fred Bowdlers not been a complete disgrace to humanity, would indeed have been the case. Thereafter, I know no more. I do not know whether they got drunk and jumped off the cliffs or whether they fell. We are rid of them anyhow."

The smirking prosecutor has real fun and games, as you may imagine, in cross-examination. He is *delighted* that Roger confesses the murderous intent of his little excursion to the seaside. What more could the Court demand, after all? As for the *little voice* that pops up and talks him out of his plan, we could all smile about that couldn't we? A pretty little fairy tale, indeed, cooked up by Roger P. in his prison cell, we can only imagine. Particularly since he has never once, never a single time, talked about this character, either to the police or to the criminal psychologist who examined him. Why, he asks Roger, has he now, faced with judge and jury and with all the evidence, including his own, pointing to guilt, why has he suddenly pulled this rabbit out of his hat? Does he imagine that anyone is going to believe him?

Emboldened by the certainty of his imminent conviction, Roger now speaks without any precaution at all. They can judge him as they wish; that's their problem, no longer his. He will tell them the truth and nothing but the truth, so help his soul.

He must not be judged, he tells the Court, on the basis of his apparent bad character. If there are members of the jury who consider that his profession as a tabloid journalist is dishonourable, he can only agree with them. The entire, shallow, scurrilous and often scabrous popular press is a disgrace to the country. Though at the time of the deaths in the case he was still employed by 'The Daily Hack', he had spiritually and morally and *intellectually* moved far out of and beyond its orbit. Yes, he had still held his job at the time, but he hoped, quite insanely, of course, that he could gradually insinuate his belief in great humanistic causes into its editorial philosophy (which, of course, was far too grand a word to employ in the circumstances.) He had failed and in desperation had sought another road to attain justice. He had been wrong but he had himself become aware of his own shortcomings. Like Socrates, his inner voice, the spectator who looked over him constantly, corrected his mistakes and drew him towards the greater truths and values available to man; he could not, in fact, have killed these men under any circumstances. It had been a fabrication and an illusion of his emotive, instinctive, unthinking self to ever imagine for an instant that he would do this.

"He stopped me. He's always stopped me. He will always stop me," are Roger's final words, as he sees at least two members of the jury stifling yawns. His case will rest there.

After summings-up which bring no new facts nor arguments, and a few legal clarifications from the judge, the jury retires to consider its verdicts.

Time to send out for some hemlock, Roger, I tell him. It's all over, you know.

As it was indeed, and as you know already: Concurrent life sentences for two murders.

Tomorrow, six months after the trial, Roger P. is being taken back to the psychologist for examination—another periodic 'assessment', I do believe they call it. The guard on the way will be light and in the psychologist's office itself, practically non-existent, as we've seen on our previous visits. I shall be leaving this manuscript here in the cell, only slightly hidden (they won't do a proper search until Roger is well away), with separate instructions on what the prison and police should do with it.

So, our story comes to an end.

I do not know whether I shall eventually be able to save Roger or not. But, of this I am sure: I shall have other work to do, much work, with other men. Socrates said that his daimonic experience had "happened to almost nobody else." That's astonishing, isn't it? But I like to be optimistic. Perhaps our species has evolved again since the time of that wise old man? Perhaps many among us now possess a compelling inner voice who will save us? And humankind into the bargain?

In any case, before I leave you, I offer these last few thoughts that I would like you to consider:

A famous cellist, by then a very old man, once addressed a peace conference at the United Nations in New York, before playing a poignant Catalan melody, 'The Song of the Birds'. With great fervour, his voice breaking with emotion, he cried: "The birds in the sky sing 'Peace! Peace! Peace!" There was not a dry eye in the house in these moving minutes, which ended with enthusiastic applause and a standing ovation. Only the cold-headed knew and thought: Right now, back home, the governments of half the delegates in this hall are enthusiastically engaged in killing their neighbours and their own countrymen in four dozen wars or civil conflicts. The hypocrisy—or simple obliviousness, if you want to be kind

—of man quite takes the breath away, doesn't it, ladies and gentlemen? These people getting sentimental about a grand old man's passionate pleas for peace could themselves have put a final stop to the carnage by the end of that week!

As for the birds ... They cry for peace? Without wishing to be churlish, I have to tell you that, alas, they do not, though they presumably have their fun-loving moments, like all of us, when they are not themselves killing something or other. The un-anthropomorphic truth about these beautiful little creatures is that they too are at permanent war, between themselves, of course, and also with any other living thing which might make an excellent lunch or has just wandered innocently into their territory. They get angry, too, these birds, and pick fights to the death, even with their own kind ...

Only recently in the long and arduous evolution of man have we come to live independently in our own minds, I believe. Until now, we have shared our cerebral space with gods from whose attention nothing supposedly escaped. At first, they were vengeful gods who demanded that we perpetrate unspeakable evils upon each other in order to please them. In time, other, more kindly deities emerged whose messengers upon earth preached love, goodness and kindness; yet we kept on torturing and killing our brothers and sisters anyhow, excusing these gods from responsibility and taking all the blame upon ourselves, and rightly so. Unlike the vengeful gods to whom we paid tribute and gave gifts, whose manifestations—tempests, eclipses, famines, poverty, disease and death—were numerous and kept man in thrall, our new gods are nowhere to be seen, are quite invisible; for we have come to understand and explain these natural phenomema. Proof of the existence of gods has disappeared entirely (even if at least one important church cooks up highly dubious tales of miraculous import from time to time). Not only do the gods continue to abstain from the prevention of man's atrocities and tragedies in our time, but they have shown themselves completely impotent to change anything at all in our lives, however minor and however much we may beg them.

The extraordinary conclusion we must inevitably come to is that man is now more powerful even than his gods, for he *can* and indeed sometimes *does* change his own fate.

I, The Spectator, tell you this in my parting words:

A vulture sweeping down the mountainside to seize a lamb stranded on a ledge, throwing it down from the cliffs to a certain death, cannot and will not stop itself. Man alone among animals can resist his instincts to torture, to maim, to kill. Only man can change what he is. Unlike the beasts of the skies, seas and forests, he is not condemned forever to be nature's slave. Nothing in man's behaviour is determined definitively; awakening and renaissance lie waiting for his embrace. Man is the only creature on this earth with complete freedom to choose what he will become. Think about it, dear readers, my friends. And peace be with you all.

About the Author

Born in 1954 in London of mixed Scottish and English parentage, Timothy Balding grew up and was educated on a British military base in Germany. He left school and his family at the age of sixteen to return alone to the United Kingdom, where he was hired as a reporter on local newspapers in Reading in the county of Berkshire. For the ensuing decade, he worked on local and regional titles and then at Press Association, the national news agency, covering politics in Westminster, the British Parliament. He exiled himself to Paris, France, in 1980, and spent the next thirty years working for international, non-governmental organizations. For twenty-five of these, he was Chief Executive Officer of the World Association of Newspapers, the representative global group of media publishers and editors, established after World War II to defend the freedom and independence of the press worldwide. A Knight (First Class) in the Order of the White Rose of Finland—an honour accorded him by Nobel Peace laureate Martti Ahtisaari, former Finnish President—Timothy Balding currently lives in the Basque region of France and devotes himself to writing. *The Spectator* is his fourth novel.

Also available from UWSP

- *November Rose: A Speech on Death by Kathrin Stengel* (2008 Independent Publisher Book Award)
- *November-Rose: Eine Rede über den Tod* by Kathrin Stengel
- *Philosophical Fragments of a Contemporary Life* by Julien David
- *17 Vorurteile, die wir Deutschen gegen Amerika und die Amerikaner haben und die so nicht ganz stimmen können* by Misha Waiman
- *The DNA of Prejudice: On the One and the Many* by Michael Eskin (2010 Next Generation Indie Book Award for Social Change)
- *Descartes' Devil: Three Meditations* by Durs Grünbein
- *Fatal Numbers: Why Count on Chance* by Hans Magnus Enzensberger
- *The Vocation of Poetry* by Durs Grünbein (2011 Independent Publisher Book Award)
- *Mortal Diamond: Poems* by Durs Grünbein
- *Yoga for the Mind: A New Ethic for Thinking and Being & Meridians of Thought* by Michael Eskin & Kathrin Stengel (2014 Living Now Book Award)
- *Health Is In Your Hands: Jin Shin Jyutsu — Practicing the Art of Self-Healing (With 51 Flash Cards for the Hands — on Practice of Jin Shin Jyutsu)* by Waltraud Riegger-Krause (2015 Living Now Book Award for Healing Arts)
- *The Wisdom of Parenthood: An Essay* by Michael Eskin
- *A Moment More Sublime: A Novel* by Stephen Grant (2015 Independent Publisher Book Award for Contemporary Fiction)
- *High on Low: Harnessing the Power of Unhappiness* by Wilhelm Schmid (2015 Living Now Book Award for Personal Growth & 2015 Independent Publisher Book Award for Self-Help)
- *Become a Message: Poems* by Lajos Walder (2016 Benjamin Franklin Book Award for Poetry)
- *What We Gain As We Grow Older: On Gelassenheit* by Wilhelm Schmid (2016 Living Now Gold Award)
- *On Dialogic Speech* by L. P. Yakubinsky
- *Passing Time: An Essay on Waiting* by Andrea Köhler

- *In Praise of Weakness* by Alexandre Jollien
- *Vase of Pompeii: A Play* by Lajos Walder
- *Below Zero: A Play* by Lajos Walder
- T*yrtaeus: A Tragedy* by Lajos Walder
- *The Complete Plays* by Lajos Walder
- *Homo Conscius: A Novel* by Timothy Balding
- *Spanish Light: A Novel* by Stephen Grant
- *On Language & Poetry* by L. P. Yakubinsky
- *Philosophical Truffles* by Michael Eskin
- *The Complete Poems* by Lajos Walder (Bilingual Edition)
- *Összes Versei* by Vándor Lajos
- *The Man Who Couldn't Stop Thinking: A Novel* by Timothy Balding
- *Of Parents and Children: Tools for Nurturing a Lifelong Relationship* by Jorge & Demián Bucay
- *The Impostors: A Novel* by Timothy Balding
- *The Zucchini Conspiracy: A Novel of Alternative Facts* by Timothy Balding
- *Drámái* by by Vándor Lajos
- *The Square Light of the Moon: A Journey of Healing with Jin Shin Jyutsu —an Ancestral Japanese Medicine* by Véronique Le Normand
- *On Writing Philosophy: A Manifesto* by Michael Eskin
- *Gespräch über Deutschland. Mit zwei Essays* by Ulrike Draesner and Michael Eskin
- *Channel Swimmer* by Ulrike Draesner

Made in the USA
Middletown, DE
27 May 2024

54921483R00130